OPERATION RED DRAGON

THE DAIKAIJU WARS
PART ONE

RYAN GEORGE COLLINS

SEVERED PRESS
HOBART TASMANIA

OPERATION RED DRAGON

Copyright © 2018 by Ryan George Collins

WWW.SEVEREDPRESS.COM

ISBN: 978-1-925711-79-0

Dedicated to my parents, Lehann and Randy Collins, who called me into the living room to see my first Godzilla movie on TV with no idea what they were starting. Thank you both for supporting me through the years.

"Canst thou draw out leviathan with an hook? Or his tongue with a cord which thou lettest down? Canst thou put a hook through his nose? Or bore his jaw through with a thorn? Will he make many supplications unto thee? Will he speak soft words to thee?"

~ The Book of Job, Ch. 41, v. 1-3 (KJV), now believed to be an early description of a Daikaiju.

PROLOGUE

December 8, 1952

Richard Godfrey had heard of Doctor Daisuke Armitage before, and even though he was fighting a cold and probably should have stayed in his dorm to rest, he forced himself out of bed to attend the doctor's seminar. This was a once in a lifetime opportunity that he simply could not miss.

Dr. Daisuke Armitage was one of the few people in the world for whom the term "living legend" was most probably literal. A Japanese-American by birth, the man was such a fantastical figure that some did not actually believe he existed, and the good doctor seemed to like it that way. According to the rumors, being regarded as semi-mythical made it easier for him to do his work, which fell into the realm of investigating, and sometimes confronting, the paranormal, or as he was known to call it, the Absurd. Some rumors even said that Armitage himself was such an Absurdity; they said he was ageless, possibly immortal, and there was even photographic evidence showing him alive and well going back to at least the early 1900s. Armitage had never denied the allegations. In fact, he had never addressed them at all, which only served to maintain the mysterious atmosphere which engulfed his life.

The seminar was exclusively for the journalism students at the university, and attendance was strongly encouraged, but not mandatory. Richard could not for the life of him figure out why a paranormal investigator would want to speak to journalism students, a collective renowned for their jaded cynicism, or why the college had agreed to let him. All he knew was that, as an aspiring journalist himself, he was naturally curious. As far as he was concerned, he had to see this Daisuke Armitage for himself.

The lecture hall was far from packed. Although it was capable of seating upwards of two-hundred people, Richard counted only twenty present, himself included. He was not quite sure if he was disappointed by this turnout or not. He supposed that would hinge on whether or not Armitage turned out to be a crackpot wasting everyone's valuable time.

The dean came out onto the stage and gave a brief introduction, in which Richard noticed a curious hint of something in his voice. To Richard, the dean sounded deeply respectful, almost reverent, as though he were introducing the Pope. So, at the very least, there were members of the faculty who took this mystery man seriously.

When Daisuke Armitage took the stage, Richard was startled by how ordinary the man looked. He was surprisingly short – or, at least, far shorter than Richard had imagined he would be – and dressed professionally but unremarkably, with a sweater vest pulled over a plain collared shirt and dress pants. The only sign of physical age about him was the dusting of gray hair on his temples and pencil-thin moustache, and his only unusual accessory was the monocle over his right eye. His expression was completely neutral, showing absolutely no indication of emotion, yet in spite of this, his eyes were exceptionally bright and alert.

Armitage stood at the microphone, and immediately began his lecture. His opening monologue was one he used often, and he knew it by rote. "It is a commonly accepted fact among philosophers that the universe is an inherently absurd place. It is also a commonly accepted fact among philosophers that commonly accepted facts among philosophers are not commonly accepted facts among regular people. This is, in and of itself, considered to be inherently absurd, thus lending credence to the commonly accepted fact among philosophers that the universe is an inherently absurd place. It is pure hyperbole, and yet it continues to build in an increasingly absurd fashion, looping back on itself like Oroborus devouring its own tail, until any philosopher who supports the idea attempts to prove that his limbs are made of elastic by putting himself on the rack, and thus becomes a philosophizing torso in a travelling carnival."

The line received a chuckle from the crowd, since the last part was intended as a joke. As Armitage continued his talk, though, it became evident that his view of the world as an absurd place was to be taken quite seriously. Throughout the rest of the lecture, he presented eyewitness accounts, films, photographs, and countless pieces of evidence pointing to the existence of monsters, aliens, and other strange phenomena that flew in the face of science and reason as man knew it, and yet were so compelling that it was hard to dismiss them. He offered little in the way of hard scientific answers, for even he, with his own extensive knowledge of science and reason, knew only so much, and he was both brave and intelligent enough to admit that.

After two hours of a presentation filled with potentially world-shattering accounts, Armitage delivered his concluding statement. "So, why have I shared this with you, students of the free press? Why not speak to the science majors or, perhaps, the fantasy writers?" His already narrow eyes narrowed even more, as if they were flashlights focusing powerful beams of light on the crowd. "I chose to speak to you for one very important reason, and you had best listen carefully and take my words to heart, for you will not hear them anywhere else. Journalism is championed as the voice of Truth, the best way to deliver facts to the public, but it is only as good as the people practicing it. Even now, I am sure that many of you doubt my words. Are there any here who think me insane? Be honest, now. I shan't judge you."

Of the twenty students, half raised their hands in affirmation.

"In that case, ask yourselves *why* you still doubt. Is it because my evidence is lacking? Or is it, perhaps, because it contradicts what you believe to be true?" He paused, letting the question sink in before continuing. "If it is the former, I invite whoever feels confident that you can to step up here and disprove me now."

He paused again, and waited. No one accepted his challenge. "If it is the latter, as it now clearly appears to be, then you must either extract such bias from yourselves, or else extract yourselves from journalism entirely. You cannot allow bias to dictate how you report, because bias is a knife that cuts Truth to shreds. All that I have shown you today should have been the biggest news stories of all time, yet they remain in the realm of what is derogatorily called 'pseudoscience' because people choose not to take these stories seriously. The people in this room are the future of journalism." Richard suddenly felt as if Armitage was staring directly at him. "Some of you may even achieve greatness one day. But whatever path your careers take, you must remember to only speak the Truth, no matter how unbelievable it may seem. If it seems too absurd to accept, research it. If your research forces you to consider altering your perception of the world, then maybe your perception was never correct in the first place. Either way, it is your responsibility as journalists to *always* report the Truth."

After the lecture, Richard neither knew nor cared how many of his classmates had been affected by the doctor's words. All that mattered was how they had affected him. He believed everything the mysterious man had said, from the absurd accounts that had comprised the bulk of the lecture to his closing remarks about bias.

That day, Richard Godfrey vowed to become a great journalist who only reported the Truth, and from that day on, he, too, would focus on the Absurd.

One week later, something very absurd happened that would eventually be significant in Richard's life. Although he was vaguely aware of the story when it was reported, thanks to the air of secrecy surrounding it, he would remain unaware of its greater impact for several years.

Two years prior in 1950, some business entrepreneurs had built a small rustic resort at the foot of Mount Fujiyama in Japan, and it had quickly become quite a popular honeymoon destination. On the resort's patio sat a hot tub, and in this hot tub sat Taizo and Akiko Tanaka, who had been married just three days prior and had arrived that morning. Their trip had been a hectic one, fraught with delayed trains and irritable cab drivers, and so after getting their bags into the honeymoon suite, they had gone to the hot tub to just relax and enjoy each other's company. They were both eager to get to certain other honeymoon activities, but there was time enough for that later. For now, the exhausted pair were content to let the churning hot water boil away the tension from their stiff muscles.

It was Akiko who first heard a low rhythmic humming that was not generated from the tub, but it was Taizo who first looked up to see the oblong craft above them. He pointed it out to his new wife.

"What is that?" Akiko asked as she looked up, squinting to keep the sun's brightness from blinding her.

Taizo also squinted as the craft descended closer to the building. "Not sure," he said. "Looks like a jet without wings."

"Maybe it's a UFO from space!" Akiko exclaimed. "Oh, wouldn't it be so exciting if aliens landed here?"

Taizo grinned. "It would be quite a memorable honeymoon."

Whatever the thing was, others at the resort had noticed it as well. Crowds were forming on the patio, the snow-covered yard, and anywhere else that provided a clear look at the object. Those who had cameras grabbed them and snapped photographs of it.

Loud static filled the air, followed by the equally loud voice of a man speaking in fluent Japanese which projected from the craft. "Attention! Attention!" said the voice. "All civilians, please evacuate the area immediately! This is an emergency! Please evacuate the area immediately!"

The message was repeated in English, yet nobody moved at the behest of either language. Everyone was too fascinated by the strange craft above them, especially now that it had spoken in two recognizable dialects. The onlookers chattered like hens, speculations flying left and right about the mysterious ship. None of them even noticed that the ground was beginning to tremble.

By the second time the message had repeated in both languages, an unearthly noise filled the air, sounding like nothing less than the ghastly roar of a demon.

The ship suddenly swerved to the side, narrowly avoiding the impact of a flaming object twice its size. This new object was not flying by its own power, but appeared to have been launched or thrown. Stranger yet, it was vaguely shaped like a dinosaur, although the flames and the way its extremities flailed about limply as it sailed above the resort pointed to it being very dead. The thing landed in a clearing on the slope, and the flames were smothered by the snow as it rolled away like a discarded, burnt ragdoll.

The sound of trees and earth splitting, overlaid with the growling of something which sounded impossibly large, washed over the crowds from the summit.

All eyes turned to where the flaming creature had come from, the mysterious craft now completely forgotten. Above the trees, they could see the upper half of a monster, its scaly skin shining as red as the fires of Hell itself, marching towards them. In the grip of its massive hands was another dinosaur-like beast, writhing and struggling in vain to halt the red giant's advance.

Few stared long enough to take in any more detail than that.

Panic ensued.

Taizo and Akiko leapt from the hot tub. The jolt of emerging from hot water into freezing winter air barely registered with either of them. They did not dry themselves or don their bathrobes. They just barely managed to slip their sandals back on before vaulting over the patio rails into the snow, clad only in wet bathing suits.

As the vacationers fled, Akiko dared to glance back. The giant was striding past the resort, its swaying tail knocking casually into the building as if the beast did not even notice it was there.

She did not stop to wonder if their possessions had been destroyed, nor did she stop to wonder what this giant was.

She just kept running.

The day after the Tanaka's terrifying honeymoon encounter, Bill Forbes was a thousand miles from civilization, hiking the Rocky Mountains all on his own.

This trip was easy for him, even in the dead of winter. The Rockies were practically his second home. He spent more time hiking the hills than doing anything else. Usually, he was a wilderness guide, but this week, he was taking some time for himself. As it happened, his wandering had taken him to a narrow valley he had never hiked before, and he would stop every few miles to map out his trail. He figured that if it turned out to be safe enough, perhaps this could be a new path to take visitors on.

The terrain on which he currently trod was most unusual. The ground was relatively smooth, and might have appeared as a flat plane to the untrained eye and foot, but Bill was aware of a very slight incline as he progressed, like what he imagined a bug might feel when climbing on an upside-down plate. Even more curious was the forest of craggy spires in this place. The spires were much taller than him, averaging at least twenty feet from base to tip, if his guess was right. He might have considered them stalagmites, given how narrow and conical they were. The problem with that notion was that he was not in a cave, nor did this area show any signs that it had once been an enclosed space.

Naturally, he had taken pictures. He knew some geologists back in town who could probably tell him what the strange formations were.

As Bill sat down by such a formation to rest his bones before continuing, the hair on the back of his neck stood up. He suddenly felt as though he were being watched.

Was somebody else there? That should have been impossible, unless someone either had followed him or was terribly lost. He doubted there were any campsites here, for he had seen no evidence of human activity beyond himself.

He glanced around, looking for any signs of life around him. From his current vantage point, he could see no one. The sand was too fine and the wind too strong for any tracks to remain for long. Even his own tracks had been swept away by the wind at this point.

It struck him that if he really was not alone, his unseen companion might not be human. It could very well be a mountain lion. That made sense, this being completely wild territory, but it also meant he could be in grave danger.

Luckily for him, he had encountered predators in the wild before, and thus had experience. He knew the best way to deal with predators was intimidation. Only the most desperately hungry beast would attack something that presented itself as too much trouble. He just had to play his cards right, and present himself as an alpha who was not to be trifled with.

As Bill stood and prepared to put on his best intimidating front, he heard a chattering noise echo through the spires which made his skin crawl. This was a new sound to him, certainly not the sort of noise a mountain lion would make, nor was it the wind howling through the valley.

This unfamiliar element put Bill even more on edge. Slowly, his eyes scanned the spires around him. His gaze settled on a very large tan boulder sitting on the smooth sandy ground about fifty feet away, though he was not sure why he was noticing it. There were many boulders here. He had passed a dozen like it without any concern.

Then it struck him that this particular boulder had not been there before.

The boulder rose off the ground, supported by eight jointed legs as thick as tree trunks. A pair of long pinchers uncurled from beneath it and reached out towards him, snapping angrily. From behind rose a large, curled appendage with a deadly-looking spike at the end that was impossible to mistake for anything but a stinger.

Bill froze as recognition kicked in.

It was a scorpion. At least, it looked like a scorpion. All of the details were unmistakable, yet Bill's mind refused to accept that this creature really was a scorpion. It was huge, bigger than a school bus, which was supposed to be impossible outside of bad monster movies. Bill remained transfixed by the sight as his rational mind refused to believe what his eyes beheld.

The scorpion took a step forward, snapping Bill from his stunned trance. He turned tail and ran, his struggle to comprehend now forgotten.

The scorpion pursued, moving much faster than he expected from something its size. If it did not need to maneuver the spires, the thing might have outpaced him easily. As it was, the scorpion was still gaining on him, and it was likely to catch up soon.

Frantically, Bill's eyes scanned the strange valley for something that would either grant him a tactical advantage or provide him an escape. As he searched, he became aware of other giant scorpions, dozens of them, crawling down the steep, craggy walls of the valley. Shock hit him when he realized that the beasts were moving in formation like a pack of wolves. He only spared a moment to realize how strange this was, since scorpions were not pack animals, but any further curious observations were dismissed when he realized in horror that they were all converging on him. They even made adjustments to keep him in their sights as he ran.

At long last, he spied salvation ahead of him: a cave in the rock face of the largest mountain. The mouth was big, but did not look big enough for the scorpions to follow him through, or so he hoped. Regardless, it was his best bet. He just had to get there before the scorpions crawling down that section of the mountain range got close enough to cut him off. He kicked into high gear, pushing himself to run faster than he had ever run before.

Dry explosions sounded behind him, and he dared to risk a glance. The first scorpion had been joined by two others, and the exploding sounds were their tails and pinchers striking the ground and spires. Maybe it was just his fear warping his perception, but it seemed like each strike was getting closer to him.

Bill pushed himself to run even faster, even as his legs began to feel numb from the exertion. He shoved all thoughts of the monsters from his mind, focusing all of his attention on the cave and the safety it promised, and was only vaguely aware that the ground was starting to rumble beneath his feet.

The scorpions were closing in. This would be close.

He dove for the cave.

He tumbled end over end.

He was stopped when his back slammed into a flat slab of rock, which knocked the air from his lungs.

As he tried to regain his breath and his senses, he could hear the snapping of pinchers and striking of stingers, but none of them were accompanied by pain. As he recomposed himself, he realized this meant that the scorpions could not reach him in the cave. He was safe, at least for the moment.

The ground continued to tremble, but Bill realized this trembling was not being caused by the scorpions. They were big, but not that big, and the ground had not shook like this during the chase. No, this trembling came from below, like an earthquake.

If it was, indeed, an earthquake, then Bill had simply traded one danger for another. He was having a very hard time deciding which of his potential fates would be worse: being eaten alive by impossibly large scorpions, or being buried alive in a cave no one else knew the location of.

As the trembling grew more violent, the scorpions retreated from the cavemouth, granting Bill a clear view of the valley outside. He watched as the ground heaved beneath the rocky spires.

He watched as the dirt crumbled from those spires, revealing them to be smooth conical spikes shining like ivory in the midday sun.

He watched as the ground actually rose up, resting on the back of some massive living thing he could not see the entirety of. Or perhaps the ground *was* its back.

He heard a terrifying, guttural roar louder than anything he had ever heard before.

Fear overtook him, and he was suddenly a child again, terrified of monsters he had not believed in for years. He turned away from the entrance in terror, covering his ears and squeezing his eyes shut as tightly as he could. This did little good, as he could still hear the scuttling of the scorpions' feet peppered with sickeningly wet crunching, and feel the repeated impact of what sounded like a dozen bombs exploding just outside. He braced himself for a cave-in, expecting each new breath drawn to be his last.

It took Bill five full minutes to realize that the commotion beyond his natural sanctuary had ceased, and the thunderous booming, which had the rhythm of footsteps to it, was growing faint.

Slowly, he opened his eyes, turned, and crept back towards the entrance, squinting as he stepped into the sunlight. Once his eyes adjusted, he was treated to a horrifically amazing sight.

The forest of spires was no longer stretched out before him. In fact, it was almost perpendicular to the ground and disappearing behind a mountain. Where it had once been, an expanse of sand and gravel now rested. It did not rise quite as high as the cave entrance, but he guessed that he could probably clamber down into it without much trouble and return to civilization. Scattered about were the scorpions, crushed and mangled as if by an enormous studded boot. In the distance, sunlight glinted off an oblong metallic object hanging in the sky like a silvery fruit.

Even through the severe shell shock brought on by the chase, Bill Forbes swore to himself that he would never return to this part of the Rockies ever again.

It would be years before he told anyone this terrifying tale, and as he expected, he was mostly met with disbelief and ridicule.

The day after Bill Forbes' harrowing fight for survival, Carlos Hernandez was flying his helicopter out over the Pacific, a few miles off the coast of Chile. He had no particular destination or goal in mind for this flight. He was simply doing a routine systems check to make sure everything was in working order. Carlos made his living as a freelance pilot for hire, flying tourists, explorers, and aristocrats with nothing better to do wherever they wanted to go in a helicopter he had purchased from the military before it could be banished to the scrap heap. This season had been slow, and so his chopper had been sitting in its hangar for long stretches of time. In order to keep it from getting too dusty, he would take it out on little excursions like this one every so often.

During this particular flight, something in the distance out over the ocean caught his eye. At first, it looked like a dark storm cloud, which was odd, since the weather report had not called for any storms that day, and the only other clouds in the sky were white and fluffy. Yet the cloud darkness which loomed ahead of him was undeniable. It swirled above a roiling patch of sea, and there were frequent bursts of bright orange flares within it.

Strange, he thought and brought his chopper to a hover. In all of his years as a pilot, he had never witnessed anything like orange lightning, nor had he ever even heard of such a thing.

He squinted. The longer he stared at the cloud, the less it resembled one. The swirling was too fast, the shape too inconsistent, and the color too dark. It looked familiar, but where had he seen something like it before? He wracked his brain, but the answer eluded him.

As both a pilot and a sane individual, he knew that flying towards a weather anomaly, especially an unusual one, was a potentially suicidal move, but he was nonetheless curious. He turned his chopper and advanced towards the cloud, resolving not to get too close, but close enough to get a clearer view and figure out what this strange phenomenon was.

Carlos drew nearer to the anomaly, and he could now pick out distinct shapes within it. He could see that the cloud was not a cloud at all, but hundreds of dark things in the air, moving in swirling patterns. From this distance, still a few miles away, the things resembled birds.

Starlings! That was what the cloud resembled: a murmuration of starlings swirling through the air in a rhythmic pattern. Yet this was impossible. Not only were starlings not native to Chile, but these birds before him were enormous. Even from where he currently hovered, it was clear that each one was at least as big as the various planes his chopper shared a hangar with, quite possibly bigger.

Burning curiosity compelled him to get just a little bit closer. The orange bursts came into focus now. They were not lightning strikes, but jets of flame, some striking things within the murmuration, some plummeting down to the churning sea. Carlos looked down at the boiling ocean, and saw large, leathery creatures bursting in and out of the waves, occasionally retaliating with fiery beams of their own. He could also now see that not all of the creatures within the murmuration were avian. Some looked bulky, like insects, yet still massive, and these moved against the swirling motion in chaotic disarray. The bird-like beasts also no longer looked exactly like birds, as the proportions of their bodies were all wrong. Whatever the bird-things were, they clearly did not like the bugs or the sea creatures.

To Carlos, it looked like a scene from prehistory, and in the blink of an eye, the scene changed.

A loud shriek filled the air, startling him from his mesmerized state. It was ear-piercing, drowning out even the pounding of the rotors, yet had a majestic quality combined with a sense of authority, like the shouted orders of a commander on the battlefield. It clearly came from Carlos' left.

At the sound, the birdlike creatures departed, sweeping away like a cloud of dust, leaving the insects and sea beasts alone. Once the last of the birds were gone, a column of flame burst from the heavens. Carlos could feel the heat even from where he sat within the safety of his cockpit.

The light was too much for his eyes. He covered them and turned, whispering a terrified prayer in his native Spanish tongue. He remembered the story of Moses and the Exodus from Egypt, a tale he had not thought of in years. God had appeared as fire in that story, including the pillar of flame that came from Heaven and led the Israelites to the Promised Land. This light was so blinding, it could only be described as divine.

Then he remembered the legends of Quetzalcoatl, the feathered serpent who descended from the sky on the rays of the sun. It was a beast the ancient inhabitants of South America had worshipped as a deity, so great was its power, and it had demanded their blood as an offering.

If the pillar of flame before him was the Lord God, Carlos was very intent on asking forgiveness for all of his sins as quickly as he could. If it was Quetzalcoatl, and the strange birds were its children, then prayers would do no good.

The heat died, and the blinding light faded. Carlos looked to where it had come down.

Thick pillars of steam billowed from the water, obscuring anything that might have been floating on the now calm surface. The sky ahead was clear. Where once monstrous beings had swarmed, now there was nothing. The flame must have incinerated them all.

Out of the corner of his eye, he caught a glimpse of the murmuration. The flying birdlike terrors were returning, and heading straight for him.

Cursing his curiosity, Carlos jerked the cyclic to the side, turning the chopper back towards the mainland. Then he pushed it to fly to safety as fast as it could go.

He glanced behind him, and he now saw the birds clearly.

No, he now realized they were not birds. They had no feathers, and many of them had long crests and horns atop their heads. Dragons, perhaps? Pterosaurs? Whatever they were, they were gaining on him.

Carlos' heart pounded furiously against his ribcage as if it were trying to escape his body and flee to shore ahead of him. He leaned forward, as if that would somehow make the chopper move faster. Still they gained.

It was no use. The winged devils would overtake him any moment now. Even so, he was too afraid to do anything but keep fleeing.

The first of the avian monsters flew past him at an alarming speed, followed by another, and another, until he was completely surrounded by them. None of the monstrosities paid Carlos any heed.

Without warning, the sun vanished.

Carlos looked up. Something large and solid was passing over him and the murmuration, but it was too low and too massive for him to tell what on earth it was.

When it passed, turbulence struck with a vengeance. The chopper wobbled in the air, the rotors striking several of the surrounding pterosaur creatures. None of them showed signs of major injury from the collisions, and they limped on without retaliating.

Carlos was not so lucky.

The rotors had been damaged by the creatures' thick hides. He could not recover in time to reach land, and would have to ditch in the ocean. Silently, he thanked God that he had remembered to attach and fill the floats before flying that day.

The creatures passed, and Carlos fought against gravity and nature to hit the water as gently as he could manage.

The landing was still hard, but he survived.

Once he had allowed himself a moment to relax, he realized that he was mercifully close to the shore, not enough to swim, but enough that someone would see him and send help. He could make out the town ahead, but he was too far away to make out any details.

He grabbed the binoculars he kept in the cockpit and focused on the town. He was relieved to see that it still stood, though the people were out and about, all eyes turned upward towards the heavens.

So others had seen the creatures. Carlos was relieved to know that. Now he could tell people what had just happened without being labeled as a lunatic.

He heard a low humming sound as his rotors stopped spinning, and looked up to see an oblong metallic object flying towards the shore in pursuit of the pterosaurs.

Well, maybe people would still think he was crazy if he mentioned that.

This was how it all began.

CHAPTER 1

April 26, 1964

"Garbage! Rubbish! Absolutely WORTHLESS!"

The Editor-In-Chief of the *Northwest Tribune*, the smallest newspaper in the entire state of Oregon, slammed the folder onto his desk with the same level of disgust and contempt he might have had for a rotting fish being served to him for dinner. Richard Godfrey flinched at the impact, and his spirits began to dwindle as the Editor followed his critiques with, "I've never read something so completely, insipidly *stupid* in my whole life!"

Richard did his best to maintain his composure as he sat across from the Editor. If he channeled his frustration at this treatment into keeping a strong, unaffected front, he might still be able to sell the article. It had worked once or twice for him before. "So…not front page material, then?" he said. It was a feeble comeback, delivered with little confidence, but unfortunately, it was hard to come up with something better under the barrage of angry insults.

The Editor erupted in loud, condescending, fake-sounding laughter that caused the rolls of fat on his body to ripple. "Front page? Are you kidding me? This tripe isn't worthy of the funny pages!" He leaned forward, his brow furrowed. "You expect me to print a story about some crazy fishmonger who says a dinosaur in the water sank his dinghy?"

Richard's anger began to boil within him again, but he channeled as much of it as he could into his clenched fists, which he kept settled on his lap. He was determined to not be dragged into a shouting match with this man. Shouting matches with newspaper editors never ended well for the reporters; this he knew from experience. Still, he had to say something in defense of his subject. "Joe Pascal is a retired Navy officer, highly decorated," he said. "Some of his friends he served with were on the boat, too. They backed him up on this."

"Oh, he was in the *Navy*, and his boyfriends are behind him? Well, stop the bloody presses!" The Editor's mocking tone grated against Richard's ears just as much as the buzzing of the printers and clicking of typewriters that were poorly muffled by the glass door to the office. "I don't care if this nutball is the latest reincarnation of the Dalai Lama! Nobody believes in this sea monster crap, and if *you* do, then no wonder you're still freelance!"

That tore it. Richard could stay calm when defending the subjects of his articles, but when someone insulted his journalistic integrity, that was when the gloves came off. It was personal now.

In an instant, Richard leapt from his seat and lunged forward, slamming his fists on the desk and meeting the Editor's gaze directly, their faces mere inches apart. "I'm freelance by *choice*, pal! I'm freelance because people like Joe need someone who'll listen to them when no one else will! Someone who'll give them a voice!"

The Editor was undaunted by the sudden display. "Some folks would call that indulging people's insanity."

"There's evidence! What about the photographs?"

"Blurry. Could be anything. A log…a canoe…a *turd*…" The Editor emphasized that last one as though he were driving a nail with a hammer.

"Or it could be the real deal!" Richard countered. "I had this analyzed by experts, and it wasn't tampered with!"

The Editor's eyes narrowed, and a look of smug triumph radiated from them like the sickening white glow of the florescent lights embedded in the ceiling. "Listen, twerp, you're not winning this one. I say your article is crap, and at the *Tribune*, my word is God's Law. Around here, we report on *real* stuff, world events like the Commies and the race riots, not the hallucinations people have on a bender at sea."

"Oh, I'm sure you take a lot of pride in it!" Richard stood to his full height, which was not much, but still taller than the blob before him. "I'm sure all twelve of your readers just adore the pretensions of this *small backwater rag* before tossing it in the fireplace or wrapping their fish in it!"

As satisfying as it was to say, Richard instantly regretted voicing his harsh opinion, especially when the Editor turned it back on him. "Well right now, I'm looking at some scrawny good-for-nothing who, just a minute ago, was hoping this small backwater rag would run his fish story, and I'm very confident that this is the last time I'll ever see him, in person or in print." He leaned back in his chair, satisfied that he had won. "Take your folder out of my office and go start your own fire with it, maybe in a steel drum down a dark alley like the bum you are."

The fight was utterly unsalvageable, and Richard knew it. As he reached for his folder, the Editor's stubby hand shot out like a cobra and shoved it away from him, spilling the contents onto the floor. "Oh dear, I'm *so* sorry," he said, his voice more condescending than what he might use for an infant.

Blinking away angry tears, Richard knelt down to collect his scattered work. He averted his gaze from the Editor, but had no doubt that the fat man was wearing a smug expression the whole time. As he did, he fantasized about slicing the tires of the fat blowhard's car, but he did not do so as he left. He would not have even if he had a knife sharp enough to do so.

Richard spent the next hour sitting outside of a café a few blocks down the road, sipping a lukewarm coffee as people bustled in and out the door, clearly all with places to be, unlike him. All he could do was stare at the folder and lament his current state of being.

Back in Fifty-two, when he had decided to dedicate his life to reporting on the Absurd, he had really meant it. For the rest of that semester, he had devoured everything he could find on the paranormal and bizarre, memorizing the terms and phenomena like an actor learning lines for a play. The choice to remain freelance was a tough one, but he found that it offered him a level of freedom that a steady job did not. Besides, most newspapers did not have a regular section for paranormal events, and one never knew what might catch an editor's eye.

He had wasted no time in getting into the thick of it when he graduated the following year. In the Fifties, America had been fascinated with UFOs, and some of his best-received articles were on that phenomenon. During this time, he had also published articles on monster sightings, and for reasons he could never quite quantify, he found that subject far more intriguing than flying saucers. Perhaps it was fueled by his childhood love of dinosaurs, or his love for the many giant monster movies released in that decade, but whatever it was, he was prouder of his monster articles than any others.

For a few brief, glorious years, he had prospered as more and more people accepted the paranormal as plausible. Even if some of the eyewitnesses were obvious crackpots, the public still devoured the stories, fascinated by the possibility of a world far stranger than what they usually believed.

Then Project Blue Book happened.

Richard had seen it for what it was earlier than anyone else. Project Blue Book was not about investigating UFOs, but debunking them. All it took was a little reasoning to realize that some of the so-called "rational" explanations they put forth were more ludicrous and unbelievable than the notion of flying saucers from Mars. It was utterly ridiculous, but somehow, it had worked. The government had convinced the nation to doubt their own eyes by feeding them explanations that only made sense because they used familiar, earthbound details. They spoke of swamp gas and weather balloons, stars and hoaxes, anything that was of a terrestrial, easily identified nature, and whatever could not be explained was simply swept under the proverbial rug and otherwise forgotten.

It reeked of a cover up, but it seemed as if nobody cared about that. People latched onto the explanations like remoras to a shark, and even forgot about the fact that quite a few UFO cases investigated by Project Blue Book were still unexplained, or that J. Allen Hynick, once an outspoken skeptical proponent of the project, had eventually become a UFO believer himself. None of that seemed to matter to the public, who would rather be spoon fed some cock and bull story about misidentifying the planet Venus than be called a crackpot for saying someone with extra letters after his name was wrong.

When the UFOs metaphorically crashed, they took everything else with them, including monsters, ghosts, and the entirety of the Absurd. Under the watchful eyes of the government, science had adopted a strict brand of dogma to rival the Catholic Church, declaring that anything which defied already-known science could not exist, as if their understanding of the universe was absolute and there was nothing left for anyone to discover.

These past few years, Richard had been having a hard time keeping his career afloat. It was not for lack of evidence or eyewitnesses, but rather because the papers simply refused to print his work because no one was willing to believe anymore. The few times he had attempted to sign on permanently with certain publications only saw him laughed out of their offices, for how could a whacko who believed in aliens and monsters possibly be counted as a real journalist?

He sighed as he closed the folder, a motion almost akin to closing the lid on a casket. "Sorry Joe," he whispered to, in reference to the man whose account was within. "It's looking like nobody wants to hear your story."

Richard brought his coffee cup to his lips, only to realize that it was empty. He rose and tossed it in the trash, then hesitated. He stared at the folder in his hand, and in his despair, strongly considered disposing of the article in similar fashion to the cup. The *Northwest Tribune* was the latest in a long line of papers that had rejected it, and he was growing weary of this pursuit, which seemed more and more futile each day. He could easily declare the story a bust and move on to something else. Something completely different. Something that had nothing to do with…

No, he thought. That would mean giving up. *He* still believed in the story, even if no one else did. There had to be someone out there who would be willing to print it, someone willing to listen, someone still willing to believe.

There just had to be.

He tucked the folder back into his case and left the coffee shop, never once noticing the sharply-dressed men in sunglasses who were watching him from across the street.

Richard had begun his walk home at a brisk pace, but as he drew nearer to the hotel, his gait gradually slowed. He only had the room booked for one more night, and after that, he had no idea where to go. This would be his third month without having sold an article, which meant the money in his bank account was nearly gone, and he would probably have to use what little was left to go back to his parents' home in Utah to regain his footing.

Again.

Richard loved his parents, who had supported him even with his odd career choice, but constantly going back to them whenever times got hard like this was starting to affect his self-esteem. It made him feel like a failure.

Perhaps he was.

He rounded the corner that would bring him to his destination, and slammed hard into what felt like a solid brick wall covered in fabric. He fell back, his bottom landing hard on the sidewalk.

Shaking his head in an attempt to regain his senses, Richard looked up at what he had run into. As the details came into focus, he revised the question from "what" to "whom", for it was a person he had collided with.

The figure looked to be at least seven feet tall, a giant by any man's standard, broad-shouldered and imposing. It – or he, apparently – was draped in a solid black trench coat that hung over his body unbuttoned, revealing a dark suit with blood red pinstripes beneath it. The suit, though nice, was covered in a network of stitches like jagged scars, as if it went through regular cycles of being damaged and repaired. His hands were covered by black leather gloves, and looked large enough to wrap around Richard's entire head. A fedora as black as night sat upon his square head at a stylish angle, the wide brim casting a heavy shadow over the upper half of his face. A scraggy, reddish-brown beard on his square jaw framed a scowling mouth, and through the shadow cast by the hat, his turquoise eyes seemed to glow as if there was light behind them.

The stranger's glowing eyes were locked right on Richard's, holding him mesmerized for a second.

"Uh, I... Excuse me, please," Richard stammered as he stood back up, dusting himself off. "I was lost in thought, so, uh... I wasn't-"

"Richard Godfrey?" asked the mysterious figure in a voice that was deep and gravelly, like the growl of a lion.

Before answering, Richard took a small step backwards, preparing to run if he had to. This man, whoever he was, projected an overwhelming aura of power and menace which terrified him. "Yes…" he said, trailing off as if to silently ask why his identity mattered to the stranger.

He thought he heard a click, and as he closed his eyes to blink, he felt a jolt of electricity surge through his body. His eyes reopened. The stranger was still standing before him, but his arm was raised now, a devilish-looking device in his gloved hand pointed at Richard's chest. The object fizzled with electricity.

Richard felt dizzy. He fell, but he did not hit the ground.

Above him, he saw the faces of several normal-looking fellows in plainclothes who had caught him. These men were all staring at the man in black, who was growling orders at them. At least, Richard thought they were orders. He was having a hard time focusing. The world was fading in and out around him. Sights and sounds were equally hazy, and he smelled nothing but electric smoke.

He was faintly aware of his legs rising off the sidewalk, maybe grabbed by someone else. He sort of heard two voices complaining that he was drooling on them.

As his eyes closed, he was vaguely aware of being carried.

Then he was aware of absolutely nothing.

CHAPTER 2

Nancy Boardwalk adjusted the antennae and checked the screen again. The image on the monitor was a bit clearer now, but still heavily distorted. She sighed angrily and smacked the television as hard as she could.

For a few brief seconds, the image was crystal clear, revealing the spiked carapace of the behemoth in brilliant detail. Then the distortion returned, even worse than it was before.

"Crap," she grumbled.

A sound like a heavy sack of potatoes being dropped onto a steel plate came from behind her. She was not startled; the sound was a familiar one at her office. She did not turn around, but continued adjusting the antennae, an activity she was growing sick of repeating and was just about ready to give up on.

"Miss Boardwalk," growled the menacing voice of her boss as he took his place beside her.

"X," she nodded in reply. Nancy was one of the few people in the world who was not, and never had been, intimidated by X. His black and red gangster attire, glowing eyes, and gravelly voice had seemed like an act when they first met, and though she now knew he was the genuine article, she had just grown used to his mannerisms. She was casual around him, almost familial in some ways, and as his right hand woman, she was one of the few people alive who could get away with such behavior. "Sounds like you kidnapped another civilian. What memories will we be erasing this time?"

"None," X replied. "That would be counterproductive this time."

Nancy instantly knew what the seemingly vague statement meant, and turned around to see the unconscious body of Richard Godfrey sitting limply in a folding metal chair, his unconscious frame slumped down on the small metal tray set before him. "This is the reporter?"

"The one and only."

"So we're really going ahead with it?"

"We have to." X gave her a wary look. "Don't tell me you're having a change of heart this late in the game."

Nancy shook her head. "Of course not. If you and the General think this is the best thing to do, I'm behind you all the way. If this goes FUBAR on us, though, Stingray will have our heads mounted in his study. Even you wouldn't come back from that."

"It'll work out. Trust me." X pointed at the screen. "Incidentally, what are we looking at here?"

Nancy turned back to the screen, her mood darkening as she once again faced the scrambled image which had been taunting her since lunch. "The cameras are on the fritz, and I can't make it any clearer than this for more than a second. If I didn't know any better, I'd say someone was jamming the signals. Best guess is that Armadagger is passing through a nuclear test site somewhere in the southwest."

"And the others?"

"Nothing. Every time the *Akira* sends out a probe, it vanishes, probably shot down. It's like they know we're trying to track them, and they don't appreciate it. In fact, I'd say that's *exactly* what's going on." She looked at X, one eyebrow raised like a wave on the ocean. "Behavior like that reminds me of just how smart they really are." She instinctively reached up and grasped the cross which hung on her necklace.

X's leather-clad hands clenched into fists while he grimaced. "Yeah... Humbling to think about, isn't it?"

Though his tone remained flat, someone who knew X well – as Nancy did – would have recognized a slight hint of terrified awe in his voice. "You know, there are times that I *really* hope the Doc is right about them," she said. Small reassurance, but it was all she could offer.

Richard groaned loudly as he slowly regained consciousness. He tried to say something, but since his mouth was dry and filled with the taste of burnt toast, all he could manage was a very lackluster utterance of, "...ugh..."

Nancy turned off the screen so it would not be a distraction and pulled up a chair opposite Richard which she plopped herself down upon. "Good morning, Sunshine," she said in a welcoming tone. "How are we feeling today?"

Richard rubbed his eyes and wiped the saliva from his chin. His head was pounding like a bass drum. He looked around, aware that he was not in front of his hotel or anywhere familiar. The room he found himself in was eerily similar to the office at the *Northwest Tribune*, but it was much bigger. The walls were covered with maps of the world, and the maps were covered with pins and labels, but what they signified, he could not even begin to guess. There were no desks, tables, or chairs, save for what he and the woman before him were seated in.

"That depends," Richard croaked in answer to the question. "Where are we? Er, that is..." He massaged his temples. "Where am I?"

"Until you get the proper clearance, that's classified," X replied flatly.

The sight of the cloaked figure jogged Richard's memory and snapped him into panic mode. He nearly leapt from his chair to run, but Nancy rose and caught his shoulders. "Calm down," she said softly but firmly. "Just sit."

The tone of her voice calmed him, as did her appearance. She was quite a beautiful woman, her face perfectly symmetrical, and her auburn hair pulled back in a smart bun. The bluish-gray suit which covered her fit body complimented the tone of her skin, creating an attractive figure to focus on. Thus, Richard did as she told him and sat back down.

"Don't be too worried," Nancy continued. "You're still safe and sound in Oregon."

X sighed loudly. "Thank you for undermining my authority in front of a civilian *again*, Miss Boardwalk," he snarled.

Nancy flashed X a Cheshire grin. "It's what I'm here for." She snapped her fingers. "Oh! Just remembered. Your mutant wife called earlier."

X's dual responses of "She did?" and "Do NOT call her that!" were so close together that he almost said both simultaneously.

Nancy's grin only grew wider at his flummoxed response. "Why not just loosen up and admit you've got odd taste in women?"

X's head craned forward as though he were a hungry vulture, his glowing eyes becoming even brighter, as though they were attempting to burn into Nancy's soul. "Need I remind you, Miss Boardwalk, that I could replace you with a brain-damaged lab rat and get better results than you give me?"

Any other man or woman might have soiled themselves in a staring contest with X, but Nancy was not even slightly phased. "You always say that, but I have yet to meet this miracle rat. Look, Chakra called while you were out shopping, said she had some updates. Go ahead and give her a ring. I'll get our reporter friend adjusted and registered."

"Make it quick," X snapped. With that, he turned sharply, which caused the tails of his trench coat to snap like whips, and marched out the door.

Nancy sat back down in front of Richard, and shrugged. "Hope that didn't give you the wrong impression," she said as reassuringly as possible. "He has this scary persona that I just love chipping away at from time to time, but usually, we work quite well together." She looked around the mostly barren room. "I suppose you'll have to excuse the lackluster decorating, too. We've been clearing this outpost of all essential equipment, which, thank God, doesn't include the piece-of-junk TV set behind me."

She extended her hand. "I'm Task Marshall Nancy Boardwalk. When Tall-Dark-and-Gruesome isn't around, I'm in charge."

Richard shook her hand, feeling a bit more relaxed now that his massive assailant was gone, but still perplexed by his situation. "Um, hi, I guess. I'm-"

"Richard Godfrey, freelance reporter, born 1935 in Salt Lake City, Utah."

The relaxation departed, replaced by tension once again. "How-?"

"We're a government agency." Nancy's brow furrowed. "Well, sort of. We're more adjacent. Well, actually…" She paused, then shrugged. "I'll explain the details later. The important thing is that we know who you are, and we know about your interest in the Absurd, monsters in particular."

Richard's eyes widened. "You've read my articles?" The realization that anyone had been reading his work recently came as a shock today, and his ego was boosted even as he was still confused by his surroundings.

"Your articles are why you were brought here. Hold still please." Without missing a beat, Nancy retrieved a strange-looking rectangular device from her pocket and held it in front of Richard's face. A bright flash blinded him for an instant, and spots danced before his eyes. When they faded, he felt something small and plastic land in his palm.

He looked to see what he had just been given. In his hand was a badge with a picture of his face on it. Next to the picture was a symbol that resembled a coiled red serpent with navy blue markings beneath it that might have been letters, but were too small for him to make out at just a glance in the poorly-lit room.

"Keep that on you at all times," Nancy said. "That's your new all-access ID badge for your stay with us. Wear it prominently so people know not to shoot you." She held up another object, about the size and shape of a pen, but with a button on the side and a small red light where the nub should have been, and placed it in Richard's other hand. "Keep this, too. It'll record audio and video of all of the important details for you. That button turns it on and off."

Richard could only sit for a moment and blink in astonishment, then finally asked the questions which he was only just managing to form with coherent words. "What is this? And how did you make this badge so quickly?"

"New technology," Nancy said, as if it were obvious. "Well, new to you, at least. We use it all the time. We might release it to the public one day. Maybe. I don't know."

Richard looked at the badge again, and examined the strange letters more closely. He now realized it was some form of Asian writing. "What's all this say? The writing looks Chinese."

"Japanese, actually. It says *Ryu no Gurren*. Roughly translated, it means Red Dragon." Nancy stood. "That's who we are: Operation Red Dragon. And we'd better get to the platform or X'll have our heads."

Before he could ask what platform she was referring to, Richard found himself being physically dragged by Nancy Boardwalk out of the room and down a featureless narrow gray hall which inclined gently upward towards a simple metal door.

Beyond that door, Richard was surprised to find himself led outside into an expansive grassy field. The building from which they had exited was deceptively small, looking like little more than a one-room shack. The only explanation he could think of for this anomaly was that the room and hallway he had woken up in was underground.

He felt uneasy now that he was outside, but he was not entirely sure why at first. He quickly determined that his unease must have had something to do with the field itself. Something about it looked wrong to him, but yet again, he could not specifically name what it was at first. There was nothing obviously wrong with it. This was just a vast grass-covered field, simple and flat.

Flat.

That was it. This field was flat. *Too* flat. Unnaturally flat. The ground beneath his feet felt too hard to be natural earth, lacking the springiness of dirt which people never notice until it is absent. It was like a football field, only instead of bleachers and scoreboards, the field was surrounded by steep mountains.

Richard silently cursed in his mind. When he had first realized he was outside, he had briefly thought that he might be able to make a break for it and run to safety, or at least somewhere he might lose these strangers, whom he was still unsure about, but that hope was now dashed. The mountains looked too steep to climb without equipment, making for an effective natural wall. There was nowhere for him to go, and even if there had been, he had no clue where he was beyond "still in Oregon". Besides, these people who had kidnapped him were feds, or something similar; trying to run might only get him in trouble, maybe even killed.

Ahead of them stood the man who had abducted him, trench coat billowing in the breeze. His solid black attire made him look like a shadow even in the bright sunlight. Instinctively, Richard tried to pull away from Nancy and run anyway, but her vicelike grip on his arm only tightened. She was unusually strong for a woman, he thought, but then again, he was not much of an athlete to begin with.

The man in black had a device at his ear and was speaking into it like a telephone. To Richard, this should have been impossible. He could see no cables or phone lines anywhere. Was it a walkie-talkie? No, it was too small, and the shape was much sleeker than he would have expected. It almost looked like something out of a *Flash Gordon* comic. Whatever it was, the man appeared to be using it for communication, and Richard could just barely discern a high-pitched voice responding through it, though he could not tell what it was saying.

"All right..." the man in black said. "Tell Ishiro we'll be there in thirty... Yes, we're heading out now... Right... I-"

He stopped, now acutely aware that Nancy and Richard were beside him. His face turned slightly red. "I, uh..." His eyes darted around as if looking for an exit or distraction. Upon finding neither, he placed his free hand over his mouth and mumbled, "Iloveyoutoo," then pressed a button that silenced the device, which vanished into his sleeve with a click.

Nancy smiled, clearly enjoying the spectacle of seeing him flustered. "How adorable!" she said, making no effort to mask her mockery.

"Shut up," the man growled.

"Oh, lighten up! We all know you're just a big softy inside!"

The giant in black turned to glare at her. He glanced briefly at Richard, then he smiled as well. It was a creepy, disturbing smile, at least as far as Richard was concerned. In fact, he never wanted to see this man smile ever again. "Keep this up, Miss Boardwalk," the man said, "and I'll share a few juicy details from *your* files with our guest."

Understanding and horror registered in Nancy's eyes. "Right, shutting up," she said quickly. Once again, her fingers clutched at her cross necklace.

The man offered a handshake to Richard. "Mr. Godfrey. We were never formally introduced. My name is X."

Richard did not take the hand, partly because it looked like it could crush his own, and partly because he was puzzled by the introduction. "X? That's it?" he said. "Like the letter?"

X shrugged. "Not really. You can't spell a lot with it, but it's who I am."

"What? No, that's not... I..." The flatness of X's reply made it impossible for Richard to tell if he was making a joke or stating a fact. He turned to Nancy. "Is he insane?" he whispered.

"No, but *'he'* has very sharp ears," X replied. "I, Mr. Godfrey, am a patriotic American. If you cut me, I bleed red, white, and blue." With another click, a ghoulish-looking knife appeared in his hand, which he raised to his throat. "Seriously. Want to see?"

Richard backed away. "Um... Thanks, but... I'll pass." He managed a fake smile which did little to hide how perturbed he was.

X shrugged. "Suit yourself." With a click, the knife returned to its holder somewhere within the sleeve of his trench coat.

Nancy tugged on Richard's shirt sleeve, drawing his attention back to her. "He's not kidding, you know," she said. "I guarantee you'll see him bleed those colors before all of this is over."

Before Richard could ask if this was some overdrawn joke they were setting him up for, the ground began to shake.

Remembering the earthquake safety lessons he had been taught as a child, Richard started to run back to the small building to stand in its doorframe. In this case, starting to run meant taking only one step, as Nancy's iron grasp once again stopped him before he could get much further.

The unnaturally flat field groaned with the rasping, scraping cacophony of stones grinding against each other. A patch of ground opened slowly like the mouth of a giant, but it was not crumbling. It simply retracted, two halves sliding away and vanishing beneath that ground which remained undisturbed.

Down in the newly-formed hole, Richard could make out a vast metallic expanse like an aircraft hangar, but any further details were blocked by the oblong craft that rose on a platform to the surface. The craft was sleek with short racing fins towards the back, and was perched upon skids like a helicopter. Yet despite being roughly the size of a passenger jet, its appearance was more comparable to a racecar than a plane, or anything else that was meant to fly.

Richard blinked in astonishment. "What... What is that?"

X marched towards the craft without a word, so Nancy responded. "That's our ride, Mr. Godfrey."

"Ride? Ride to where?"

"Japan." Nancy gave him a friendly pat on the shoulder. "Your latest assignment requires a bit of travelling abroad."

At this point, Richard was still confused and worried about the situation he had somehow wound up in. His desire to know what was going on did not override his desire to return to some sense of normalcy.

Then again, his reporter's instincts were screaming at him to stop panicking and consider just what he had fallen into. This day had begun as one of the worst days of his life, filled with self-doubt and despair, and now he was in the company of a government agency with advanced technologies at their disposal. Strangest of all, it seemed as though they *wanted* him to be there. Nancy had even said this was an assignment.

To Richard, "assignment" was an understatement.

This, potentially, was the scoop of the century.

He boarded the craft.

CHAPTER 3

Michael Sun hated Groom Lake.

Specifically, he hated how limited his movement was there. He was used to having free reign of government facilities, like he did back in Washington. That was part of how he did his job. Yet at Groom Lake (or whatever the suits were calling it now), he was only allowed access to certain areas. It seemed ridiculous to him. Just knowing that this place even existed was a privilege in itself, he knew, but only being allowed in four or five areas of such a big facility – including the cafeteria and the men's room of each building – was so restrictive that he may as well have been in prison. Given how much he already knew about what was going on in the world, the restrictions seemed unnecessary. He felt like a child being told where he was not allowed to go by overprotective parents, and the condescension that came from certain people who worked here really grated on his nerves.

He had caught glimpses of things through closing doors and schematics left on desks by careless workers. He did not know for certain what most of them were, but he was told that he would eventually be granted access to other areas one day, assuming everything went smoothly. He knew better than to place any chips on that square.

At the moment, he was headed to one of the few places he did have clearance to enter: Hangar 90. He was allowed there because it directly related to his work, and it was where Colonel George F. Stingray was waiting for him.

He entered through the simple sliding metal doors, and was greeted by the sight of the Colonel, illuminated by a large but dim overhead lamp and the sporadic sparks of construction. He was leaning on the balcony guardrail, staring at a towering machine the mechanics had been working on since last year. Sun could not decide which of the two looked more ridiculous. Stingray made it a point to style himself after his hero and idol, General Douglass MacArthur, and Michael had never seen the Colonel without aviator sunglasses obscuring his eyes, even at night or in the dim lighting of Hangar 90. How Stingray could always see what was happening around him was beyond Michael's understanding.

As for the machine, its mighty metal frame was still having the last finishing touches put on it, but the face was complete. He saw no reason why a machine would need a face at all, but robotics was not his field. As a Chinese-American, he appreciated the eyes, even if Professor

Toshiro, the brains behind the device, did not have China in mind when he designed them. The eyes were fine, but the goofy smile was off-putting. Why on Earth had he included that? Did he think it was funny? Was it meant to be friendly? If that last one was the intent, it was a failure. The smile was not friendly; it was creepy.

Michael stopped beside Stingray. "Good evening, Colonel Stingray," he said as if he were simply greeting a coworker at a nine-to-five job.

"Something new, Mr. Sun?" the Colonel responded in a more serious tone, his gaze never wavering from the machine.

All business, then. Just once, Michael wished that someone would open by asking how his day was going, or maybe asking if he'd seen some recent sporting event. "Well, my contact told me that X and Boardwalk have someone new with them."

Even though Stingray turned his head in Sun's general direction, it seemed like his eyes remained fixed on the machine. "Who?"

"Not sure yet." Michael looked down. Hangar 90 was not like other hangars. It went down instead of out, deep into the depths of the Earth. It was the only way this robot could be built ready-to-launch. "Don't worry, though. I can make contact again once everyone is onboard the *Akira*."

"They're heading for the *Akira*? Hmm." Stingray tapped the rail in thought. "What are they up to, I wonder?"

"If I had to guess, we're approaching a major event, and somehow, this new guy is connected."

Stingray sighed. "Once everyone's onboard, give those jokers a call. Remind them of their place."

It was Michael's turn to sigh. *That* conversation again. Every time the Red Dragons went off book, it fell on him to give them a stern talking to, not that it ever made them stop. Reminding them of their place was an exercise in futility. "Fine," he grumbled. "Assuming this *is* a major event, though, you really think this oversized toaster will be done in time?"

"If Sigma says it'll be ready, it'll be ready."

Michael nodded, and waited for a moment. When the extended silence made it obvious that Stingray had nothing else to say to him, he left.

Richard was still having a hard time believing that the vehicle he was in could really fly, even as he watched the world pass by far beneath him through a small, round window not unlike the kind he had seen on Navy ships.

"Not bad, eh?" asked Nancy, who had just sat down with a Shirley Temple in one hand and a glass of water in the other. X was somewhere else on the ship, and that suited Richard just fine.

Richard nodded as he took the water. This was, indeed, an impressive craft. The interior was spacious and comfortable, equipped with all the amenities one might need for a long flight, including reclining chairs, several TV sets embedded in the walls, and the wet bar where Nancy had gotten the drinks. Although he remained seated, the cabin was arranged in a way that made walking about remarkably easy. This was close to what he imagined the inside of a luxury hotel looked and felt like. Not only that, but the flight was remarkably smooth. If not for the evidence outside his window, he would never have guessed that they were flying at all.

He could only imagine what the people below must think the ship was. It was flying fairly high, and had reached the ocean half an hour ago, but it had flown over at least one town on the way. To an earthbound spectator, the craft probably looked like a...

Wait...

Richard started to say something, then remembered the strange metal stick he had been given, the one Nancy said was a recording device. He still had no clue how it could do what she said without a tape reel, but he also had no clue how the aircraft he sat in could fly. Ergo, if the ship could fly, the stick could record.

Besides, if there was one thing he had gotten used to as an investigator of the Absurd, it was having faith that the crazy things people told him were true.

He retrieved the device from his pocket, switched it on, and asked his question, having mentally shifted into journalist mode. "When I first saw this ship," he began, "it looked familiar to me, but I couldn't put my finger on why at the time."

Nancy cocked an eyebrow toward the ceiling, intrigued. "I assume you have a theory?"

"I was just thinking that we might look like a UFO from the ground. I've covered UFO stories in the past, and I just remembered seeing quite a few photographs of something that looks like this ship." Richard gestured to the rest of the cabin as he spoke. "It seems obvious to me now that a ship like this must be what was photographed."

"Huh," Nancy responded with the same level of enthusiasm she might have had upon being told a recipe for chicken parmesan. "I guess some of our pilots got careless. Probably Nelson, the fat dolt. Good thing we demoted his giant behind down to janitor."

Richard glanced back out the window. "So, that's the ultimate answer, then? All the UFO sightings are just classified experimental ships like this one? They're all terrestrial craft being used by this Red Dragon group?"

Nancy shrugged. "Well, some of them are. Let's just say for now that every ship you're about to see was built on this planet, and we Red Dragons are all human." She sipped her drink. "Well, we're all from Earth, at least."

Before Richard could ask for further elaboration on this strange statement, a string of yellow lights along the ceiling blinked, and a soft ding was heard. "Attention, all passengers," said a friendly female voice on the intercom. "We will be docking in three minutes. Please keep your seatbelts fastened until we have landed. Thank you, and good day."

As he clicked the latch of his seatbelt into place, Richard looked out the window again. He could see nothing but ocean and sky stretching into the horizon.

He turned back to Nancy. "Where are we going to land, exactly? In the ocean?"

Nancy placed her empty glass on the tray beside her chair and stood. "You can't see it from here. Come on." She turned and started to walk toward the cockpit.

"But, the voice just said-"

"She always says that. It's her job. Docking with the *Akira* always goes smoothly. We've been using this model of shuttle for five years and haven't had an incident yet. Come on, you'll definitely want to see the *Akira* while we're landing."

Even though it went against everything he had ever been told about flight safety, Richard unplugged his seatbelt and followed Nancy, wondering if he had heard her right, and if so, what "docking with the *Akira*" meant.

The cockpit was more like something out of a Sci-Fi movie than a proper airplane, but this futuristic aesthetic was starting to make sense to Richard by this point. The control panels did not have as many dials and gauges as he had seen in other aircraft, and the controls held by the pilot and co-pilot were both fairly small and looked like they were made of plastic. They reminded Richard of steering wheels from toy cars, the kind children sat on and moved either with pedals or their feet like the Flintstones did. The pilots themselves wore silver-colored vinyl jumpsuits and what appeared to be motorcycle helmets.

All of these details, though fascinating, paled in comparison to the object revealed beyond the large windshield.

It was another ship, of that he was certain, but it was much, much larger than the tiny craft he currently rode in. Indeed, it was massive, and the closer they got, the less he could see of it, so he tried to take in as many details as possible.

Like his current transport, this new ship was oblong, but he could not decide if the hull reminded him more of a boat or a submarine. The fact that it looked like a seafaring vessel at all was surreal, since it was floating at least a hundred feet above the water. Its nose was a rounded cone, which was the only thing about it that looked remotely aerodynamic. The rest looked very industrial. Its fuselage appeared to be very thick, and the angle of the sun made it difficult to tell if it was dark gray or dark brown. Protuberances like backwards shark fins rose from the top and sides, each supporting a disc-shaped object at the end covered in glass panels. Perhaps, he reasoned, they were observation decks. Massive rocket engines stuck out of the back, and ripples of heat beneath the ship indicated more on the underside of it. A slightly raised area behind the nose cone was lined with windows that glowed yellow from within, and Richard assumed that area might be the bridge. Along the side, large red symbols were painted. They resembled the kanji on the Red Dragon card, but he recognized none of them.

"What does that say?" he asked. He had a guess, but he hated to make presumptions. It was a habit he had dropped long ago, as a reporter who jumped to conclusions was doomed to print inaccurate stories.

"*Akira*," Nancy answered. "That's the name of our noble battleship and mobile base of operations. The good ship *Akira*." She swelled with pride upon saying the name a second time.

It was a pride Richard could understand. Industrial though it might have appeared, the ship was a magnificent sight to behold.

*****

The docking process went so smoothly that Richard hardly felt any difference from when they were flying.

As he followed everyone else down the exit ramp, he found himself within a massive golden hangar. Along the walls, arranged in neat little rows, were other small ships similar to the one which had brought them here. Men and women dressed as mechanics – he could not count how many, but he guessed there were likely more than a hundred – scurried about like drones in a beehive, tending to the various ships. He noted a distinct mix of races in the hangar, predominantly skewing towards Asian-looking people.

Directly before them stood two Japanese men, one of whom took a single step forward. He wore a pristine white military jacket adorned with medals, and a matching cap adorned with gold embroidering. His face showed a few wrinkles, and the hair on his temples was graying slightly, but his eyes shone with the vitality of a young, energetic man; in fact, his eyes seemed to glow in similar fashion to X's eyes. He stood bolt upright as though his spine were a solid iron rod, and his hands were clasped behind his rigid back. He immediately struck Richard as a very noble, distinguished, proper man.

The fellow behind him was dressed in khakis and had a distant, unreadable expression on his face. He remained completely motionless. The tightness of his lips and obvious clenching of his jaw made it seem like he was very deliberately keeping his mouth closed.

X stopped right in front of the well-dressed man. "General Tsujimori," he said curtly.

"X," was the equally-curt reply.

"Traitor," X shot back.

"Freak," the response.

"Fascist."

"Nationalist."

"Slant-eye."

"Gaijin dog."

How much longer the verbal tennis match might have lasted, and who might have won, was a question that would remain unanswered that day, as the hangar suddenly echoed with a girl's voice shouting X's name as excitedly as if he were a member of the Beatles.

The owner of the voice sprinted across the entire hangar with blinding speed and wrapped her outstretched arms around X's towering figure like a pair of especially affectionate boa constrictors. Even under the shadow cast by his fedora, everyone could see X's face turn beet red with embarrassment.

Richard could not take his eyes off the girl and how strange she looked. She seemed awfully young – if he had to guess, she could not have been much older than twenty – and although she was obviously Japanese, her eyes were large to the point of being cartoonish, and had an odd glow to them similar to X's and the General's. Her hair was cropped short and shimmered a rich, deep shade of green, yet the color looked natural as opposed to being dyed or a wig. Oddest of all were the brown canine ears atop her head, and the matching tail that stuck out from beneath her shockingly short skirt. His first instinct was to assume that these attributes were part of a costume, since he had heard that Japan had strange trends in fashion, but as he watched the ears twitch and the tail wag excitedly, he realized – yet still had a hard time accepting – that they were real.

The girl buried her face in X's chest, which was as tall as she stood. "Oh, X, I missed you *soooooooooooooo* much!" she squealed.

X slowly raised one of his restricted arms at the elbow and patted her awkwardly on the back. "Nice to see you too, Chakra," he mumbled.

The girl, Chakra, squealed again, her tail wagging even more furiously, flicking her skirt side to side as it went.

The well-dressed Japanese officer, whom X had referred to as General Tsujimori, allowed himself a satisfied grin at X's embarrassment before clearing his throat loudly. "Chakra-chan," he said, his voice carrying authority. "Why are you not at your post?"

The authority either did not register with Chakra, or she deliberately ignored it. "I hate watching the radar! It's *boring!*" she whined. "Besides, I wanted to get a look at the reporter." She released X and approached Richard, who was still staring at her. She looked him up and down, then snorted. "Looks like a pansy to me. You Italian?"

Richard blinked at the strange question and stammered a response. "Huh? Ital-uh... No..."

"Could've fooled me with those linguine arms." In the blink of an eye, Chakra was back at X's side, her arms once more wrapped around him, her voice switching back to a tone dripping with affection. "Not like you, X. You're big and strong and handsome."

X swallowed loudly, his stoic expression on the verge of breaking. "Chakra," he said in a quiet, tense voice as he blinked sweat from his eyes, "there are people watching. As much as I appreciate the affection, could you *please* tone it down a bit?"

Chakra slowly slid her arms away so as to maintain contact for as long as possible, and looked up at X with bedroom eyes. "I get it," she said, her voice adopting a sultry tone. "You want me to save it up for later, when we're alone." She walked her fingers up X's arm. "You save up some of your strength too, stud muffin." She gently touched the tip of his nose with a playful, "Boop!"

She strutted away, her hips and tail swaying like a bell in the Notre Dame Cathedral.

X saw the General smile mockingly. He straightened his now ruffled coat. "You're just jealous," he grumbled.

Richard turned to Nancy. "Who-"

"That was Chakra," Nancy replied.

"She-"

"-Has dog ears and a tail, yes."

"They-"

"-Are real."

"How-"

"Not now."

Why she was not answering became apparent when she pointed at the General, who was now standing right in front of Richard. It was strange, he thought, that this man was being called a general when his attire was that of a navy admiral, but then again, that was most certainly not the strangest thing he had encountered today.

"Richard Godfrey, I presume?" the General asked.

When Richard nodded, he continued. "I am General Ishiro Tsujimori of the Glorious Imperial-"

"Ah-HEM!!!" The sound came from X, who shot the General a dirty look.

The General sighed. "*Formerly* of the Japanese Army. You know, back when it still *existed.*" There was vitriol in the way he spoke the last word. He motioned to the man in khakis. "This is my right hand, Captain Hirata Catigiri."

Catigiri bowed, but said nothing.

"On behalf of the Red Dragon Operation," Tsujimori continued, "I welcome you aboard the *Akira*, my flying fortress."

"*Our* flying fortress, if you don't mind!" X snapped. "Don't forget that this is an international group, Ishiro."

Tsujimori turned to glare at X. "Don't forget that this ship was designed in Japan."

"And built in America."

"Well, that wouldn't have been a problem if we still had a working economy and military, but since we can't have nice things like *some* countries…"

Nancy stepped forward, her hands raised in the hopes of quelling the bickering. "Gentlemen, gentlemen," she said as if talking to squabbling children. "We can measure which country has a longer peninsula later. Let's not give our guest the wrong idea. We are a united front, yes?"

Though the argument ended, Tsujimori and X wore expressions that told of their intent to resume it another day, as they often did. "Anyway," Tsujimori said, turning back to Richard, "welcome aboard."

He offered his hand to shake, and Richard was confused to see it clad in a tight purple rubber glove. As he took the General's hand, he felt the hair on his arm stand on end. He observed the man carefully as he quickly broke the handshake and left.

There was static electricity in the air around Tsujimori, though where it was coming from, Richard could not begin to guess.

"Come on," Nancy said, pulling him from his thoughts back into the hangar. "I'll show you to your room. It's not much, but it's a place to have all to yourself."

Richard noticed some of the workers carrying suitcases off the shuttle, and realized they were his. They must have packed his things without him knowing, probably while he had been unconscious. That made it clear he was in this adventure for the long haul, whatever it turned out to be. He may have had no clue where he was or where he was going, but at least he would have some amenities.

He yawned, suddenly realizing how incredibly tired he was. "Thanks. I could use the rest after a day like this. I definitely need time to process all of this…this weirdness."

Nancy smiled. "Oh, Richard, the weirdness is only just starting."

Richard had no idea how things could possibly get much stranger, so for the sake of being able to sleep peacefully that night, he chose not to read too deeply into Nancy's retort. Then again, he was not sure he would be capable of sleeping at all after a day like this.

When he got to his room, fatigue set in, and he crashed hard onto his bed.

Thanks to the experimental technology used in its construction, video calls and text messages could be made and received just about anywhere on the *Akira*, with the exception of toilets and showers, because no call was important enough to interrupt those activities. For calls that fell under Class-A Security – the highest possible level, which only X and General Tsujimori could take (or, in their absence, Nancy and Hirata) – there were specially secured, soundproofed rooms that required passage through sophisticated security systems to access. There was one such room on every deck of the *Akira*, all located towards the front of the ship.

These rooms were also incredibly cramped and unbearably hot, as if whoever designed them wanted the occupants to be as uncomfortable as possible. Such was the price of international security, not to mention keeping so many different machines running in such a closed space.

In such a room, someone was contacting Michael Sun in America, letting him know that Richard Godfrey was aboard the ship. This someone was instructed to keep a close eye on Richard, but to otherwise not interfere just yet.

Richard Godfrey would likely have to be terminated if he posed a security threat, but not until it was necessary.

CHAPTER 4

The *Akira* flew through the night, passing a small, unremarkable island at around midnight. This island was not on any maps, and being a fairly new landmass, it had no signs of life anywhere upon it.

Beneath it, however, things were different.

The bugs had found this island only recently, and their master recognized its value. It was close enough to the larger land masses that travel would be fairly easy, yet far enough away that the tiny human creatures would not be concerned by it until it was far too late.

This made the close passage of the flying object disturbing.

Although the others of their kind had encountered it in the past, the bugs did not quite understand what the flying object actually was. Only their master could really comprehend it, but he possessed a mind equal only to a few who walked the Earth. The bugs knew the flying thing was sort of shaped like a log that burned on one end, but logs were not supposed to fly, nor were they supposed to be made of stone. All they knew was that the small human creatures, particularly the dangerous ones, went inside of it to move across the ocean.

The bugs hated the little human creatures quite passionately. The human creatures were the ones who stood in the way of them reclaiming the Earth. This hatred was something the bugs had in common with their former enemies, the reptiles, and it was enough to warrant an alliance...at least, until the humans were gone.

If only they were easier to exterminate, the planet would have been reclaimed long ago.

The flying object passed by without incident. Apparently, the tiny human creatures were as unaware of the bugs' presence on the island as they had always been.

Even so, an opportunity had presented itself, and their master refused to let it slip past him.

The tiny human creatures weren't the only ones who could fly, after all.

Chakra was having a very hard time staying awake. Not that there was much reason for her to try. Of all the jobs on the *Akira*, radar operator was the most boring one she knew. She would take janitor over this any day. At least then she could go wherever she wanted to on the ship, maybe overhear juicy details of people's lives and covert missions while she pretended to sweep the floor, and occasionally get a buzz from the chemical fumes. But no, she was stuck on the bridge, surrounded by a dozen other men and women seated at their own control panels, far removed from where the exciting stuff would happen.

That was another part of the problem. Everyone else on the bridge was actually doing something that kept the *Akira* flying. Chakra, meanwhile, was just sitting there, surrounded by the bridge's gold-colored walls that created the illusion of soft light, watching a glowing line swirling around a dark green circle over and over and over and over, waiting for things that weren't guaranteed to even show up.

Any idiot could do this stupid job. She wanted to do more. By rights, she *should* have been doing more. She had been designed to do more.

Not helping her exasperation was how tired she was. She loved X enough to have married him not long after they first met, and she loved the nights they spent together, but sometimes those nights saw the two of them staying up very late, and she had to be at this boring post really early in the morning. She had hardly gotten any sleep, and she was paying for it now by drifting in and out of consciousness at her post.

She smiled as she thought back to the previous night, and a happy sigh passed through her lips. Despite her frustration, it had definitely been worth it.

Though she did not remember falling asleep, a light bleeping noise worked its way into Chakra's sensitive canine ears and woke her. She snorted, shook her head – an action that, in true canine fashion, traveled down her body and exited through her tail – and wiped the drool from her chin and the radar screen. Chakra was many things, but a graceful sleeper was not one of them.

Indeed, there was a blip on the radar, some fifty nautical miles away, closing in fast. It registered as a bright shade of lime green against the dark tint of the screen.

Then another blip appeared beside it.

And another.

And another.

Within seconds, there were too many to count.

She checked the signatures. They all came back green.

Chakra smiled in spite of herself as her tail wagged. She knew from countless prior experiences that the blips were enemy targets who had every intention of attacking and destroying the ship, but that meant action. There were too many for the *Akira* to deal with, even with all of its weaponry. The ship would easily be overwhelmed by the encroaching swarm.

That meant X and the General would have to take care of the attack. Maybe she could join them this time.

She slammed her fist on the large red button beside her station, setting off the warning klaxons, and switched on her intercom microphone. "Incoming bogies at eight o'clock!" she exclaimed in a chipper tone that contrasted starkly with the approaching danger. "Signatures confirmed green! ETA ten minutes! Charge cannons, or else we'll all die horribly! Those of us who can, at least!"

With that, she leapt from her seat and ran off the bridge before anyone could stop her. Not that Chakra abandoning the radar came as a surprise to anyone. She did this all the time. Despite how reckless it was for her to do, especially in an emergency, the bridge crew had gotten used to it. Whoever was sitting next to her usually wound up covering her post in addition to his own. That she kept doing this without any serious repercussions did not endear Chakra to many of the bridge crew, but they knew nothing was to be done about it either.

Chakra ran as fast as she could through the *Akira*'s winding halls, knowing exactly where she was headed. If she made it in time, maybe X would let her join the fight. If not, she would probably wind up stuck on one of the observation decks again.

Either way, she had no intention of missing this.

At first, Richard thought the blaring klaxon was being made by his alarm clock, and he would wake up in his apartment in Oregon and realize that whole experience with those Red Dragon people had been nothing more than a crazy dream fueled by something strange he had eaten last night.

He dispelled this thought rather quickly. The klaxon was far too loud to be his regular clock, and once the sleep had been rubbed from his eyes, the room he found himself in was neither his hotel room nor his parent's house, but the single cabin Nancy had brought him to.

So it definitely was not a dream, and he still had no clue what he had found himself roped into.

Though a still small voice in the back of his mind was screaming at him to act with urgency, since klaxons usually signified danger of an immediate nature, he rose slowly and groggily, more annoyed by the noise than anything else. He had no idea what the klaxons meant. Maybe it was a regular function of the ship. For all he knew, it *was* an alarm clock, a way to make sure the crew had no choice but to be awake for duty.

Richard looked out the small round window beside his cot. The sun was just starting to peek above the horizon. He groaned. Even supposing that this was a military vessel, what could possibly be so important on the ship that it required everyone to be up at the literal crack of dawn?

His eyes adjusted, and he saw movement. Dozens of tiny dots, visible even in the dim light, floating through the air, growing slowly bigger, like distant objects drawing nearer.

He rubbed his eyes again. The dots did not vanish, but continued to grow. So it was not an illusion caused by bleariness. Whatever they were, they were real.

To Richard, it looked like they were flying in formation.

With that realization, Richard snapped wide awake. Klaxons plus objects flying in formation almost certainly meant action of some sort.

He leapt from his bed and ran for the door, not even bothering to change out of his pajamas. That would just waste time, and if something big was about to happen, he had to be there. Journalism took precedence over fresh clothing and fashion sense.

He stopped short of exiting, then rushed back to his bed. He reached over it towards the side table, grasping the small recording stick and the badge. He fumbled with them in his excitement, but got a firm grip on both items as he bolted out the door.

He had no idea what he was about to bear witness to, but given his current surroundings, he had no doubt whatsoever that it would be unlike anything he had ever seen before.

Neither General Tsujimori nor X had wasted a moment. The instant the klaxons began and Chakra made her call, they were up and ready. It was a habit they both had developed over years of military service.

They met before the special elevators which allowed for direct hull access. Security on this elevator used specially developed thumbprint scanners that were keyed exclusively to X and Tsujimori, making them the only ones on the whole ship who could access it. Then again, they were the only ones on the whole ship who ever needed to.

Above the sliding doors hung a sign that read "HULL ACCESS SHAFT – FOR USE BY SUPERMEN ONLY!!!" in both English and Japanese. One of the workers who had built the *Akira* had put that up as a joke, but it was accurate nonetheless.

The doors opened once both men pressed their thumbs to the scanners, and they stepped towards the opening at the same time. They stopped before colliding and paused, each waiting for the other to make the first move.

Tsujimori made a sweeping gesture towards the door. "Please, after you," he said. "You Americans love charging blindly into battle, if Korea and Vietnam are any indication."

X's nose twitched at the comment, but he shot back instantly. "Remind me again, what do your pilots do when they run out of bullets? Kamikaze means 'nose dive into the ship', right?"

"Age before beauty, I think."

"What's wrong, Ishiro? You turning even more yellow?"

They might have continued, but a voice on the intercom – which was not Chakra's, meaning she had abandoned her post yet again – reminded them that the bogies were drawing closer.

X knew exactly what Chakra's absence meant, so he had to be quick.

He stepped onto the elevator first, and the General followed close behind.

As they rode to the top, the banter resumed.

"How about following my lead this time?" Tsujimori said. "I am the better strategist, after all."

X laughed dryly. "Of the two of us, which one can fly?"

Chakra turned the corner just in time to see the elevator doors close.

She stamped her foot as her ears flattened angrily against her head. Too slow *again*. She was sure X and the General would have still been throwing insults at each other like they always did. They must have cut things short when they heard her replacement, which also meant X had already issued orders to lock down the hangar.

Crap.

She knew X was protecting her by acting this way, and it was as sweet as it was frustrating.

She tapped her fingers against the nearest section of wall as she pondered what to do next.

Well, no reason she couldn't still watch the fight, and she knew the best seat in the house.

Richard had met Nancy in the gold-colored hall mere feet from his room, and she had led him to one of the *Akira*'s three observation decks, this one located near the back of the ship. Based on the flat discoid shape of the room, Richard guessed (correctly) that this was atop one of the reverse shark fin protuberances he had seen yesterday. The room itself, which was about ten feet in diameter, was completely empty, the only accoutrements being a metal railing before the massive picture windows that lined the wall. It provided a nearly-panoramic view of the outside, including the top of the mighty flying fortress. The sound of the rockets was noticeable, but muffled by the thickness of the glass and walls.

Nancy gave Richard a pair of binoculars, and pointed out the window. "They should be coming from over there."

"Who are 'they'?" asked Richard as he raised the binoculars. "Is it the Russians? Are we in their airspace?"

"A few of them have shown up in Russia before," Nancy replied with a hint of a smirk, "but I doubt they're the same ones from then."

Richard was starting to grow weary of Nancy's cryptic responses, but before he could ask for clarification, he saw the truth with his own eyes.

Through the binoculars, he could see them clearly, riding out of the rising sun like the Valkyries of Norse mythology, but these were not Valkyries. These things would have made the Valkyries turn tail and run.

They looked like rhinoceros beetles, the kind he remembered seeing in high school textbooks. Glints of metallic blue and green shone on their shells as they flew, and each had nasty-looking horns jutting from their heads like the lances of charging knights, but what struck him most of all was the size. For them to be visible from so far away, they must have to have been huge, at least the length of a jet fighter.

And there were hundreds of them.

Richard was rendered speechless as he remembered a report he had done back in Fifty-nine. He had interviewed a family who said their car had been attacked by a giant insect of some kind. A wasp, if he recalled it correctly. He was the only person they had spoken to who believed them.

Yet even belief had not prepared him for the shock of actually *seeing* such creatures in the moment, plain as day before his eyes. The rational piece of his brain that always remained skeptical so as to rule out hoaxers and crackpots quietly slinked away and locked itself in a closet as stunned awe took control of Richard's train of thought.

Nancy noticed the huge smile spreading across his face. "You see 'em?" she asked.

Richard nodded. "They're real," he whispered, stunned. "The giants do exist." He turned to face Nancy, and excitement filled his spirits to the brim. "They're real! All this time I've investigated monster sightings, but I never saw one myself. I- I always had to go on pure faith that they existed, but now..." He grabbed Nancy by the shoulders. "I was right to believe! They're real! They're really real! Oh, what I'd give for a camera!"

"We have cameras all over the ship, recording every detail," Nancy said. She did not seem as amazed as Richard did. "We'll get you whatever footage you need, and we guarantee crystal clarity. No blurry black-and-white Polaroids. The device I gave you has a camera on it, too, if you'd prefer that."

Richard snapped his fingers as he remembered the device. He whipped it from his pocket, switched it on, and looked back out at the approaching bugs. "What do you, um... Do they have a name? Like, a species, or something?"

"The Latin name is nearly unpronounceable. We just call them Herc-Rhinos. Herc as in Hercules. I never really liked that name myself, but no one's come up with a better one yet."

Chakra appeared from the entrance, pushing between Richard and Nancy as she entered. "Did I miss anything?" she asked as she leaned on the rails, catching her breath from running.

Nancy shook her head. "Not yet," she said, then added, "Miss the lift again?"

Chakra's ears drooped as she scowled. "Yeah," she said.

Following close behind Chakra was Captain Catigiri, who nodded to Richard in acknowledgement as he entered.

"Oh...Hi," Richard said in response, not really knowing what else to say beyond that.

Something about the way the Captain stared at him without saying a word made Richard feel very awkward. He was overcome by the desire to say something in the hopes of dispelling the sensation. "You're, uh... You're Captain Hirata Catigiri, if I recall. Am I remembering that correctly?"

Hirata nodded, but said nothing.

"So, what do you do on this ship?" Richard asked.

Hirata half-shrugged and remained silent, but looked at Richard with an expression that conveyed a sense of coy amusement.

Richard felt even more awkward. "Um... Sorry if this sounds rude, but, uh, can you actually talk?"

Hirata stared at Richard as though he were mulling over how to respond, then stepped past him to look out over the hull of the *Akira* without saying a word.

Nancy patted a confused Richard on the shoulder. "Don't take any of that personally," she said. "He's just..." She paused as she searched for the right descriptor. "He's quiet."

Richard shrugged. It was not a great explanation, but with everything else he had to pay attention to at the moment, it would have to suffice until later. He went to the window and stood beside Chakra.

"Stop crowding me, you oily-haired swish," the dog-eared girl snapped, a hint of a growl in her voice.

Richard blinked, taken aback by the reception, and looked back at Nancy with a bewildered expression.

"*That* you can take personally," she said.

As Richard shifted away from Chakra, a thought struck him. The family who had seen the giant wasp said it had attacked them. "These Herc-Rhinos," he said. "Are they hostile?"

As if on cue, bolts of bright pink light shot from the bugs' horns and struck the ship, rocking it violently.

Question answered.

In response to the attack, panels on the *Akira*'s hull opened to reveal gun turrets, which rose out quickly and began firing continuous streams of anti-aircraft rounds at the attacking insects. The staccato blasting rattled the ship as thin wisps of smoke drifted from the barrels with each new burst.

Some of the bullets found their marks, obliterating their targets in a spray of sickening yellow slime, but most of them sailed off into the distance without hitting a thing.

Even as he was drawn in by the rhythm of the guns and the brightness of the bugs' attack, Richard noticed from the corner of his eye something moving across the massive gray-brown panels of the *Akira*'s surface.

He glanced down, and saw that the something moving was actually two somethings moving.

People.

General Tsujimori and X.

"What the-" he half-exclaimed, his brain not quite grasping what he was seeing, since it made so little sense. "Are they-? What are those two doing out there?"

Chakra squealed excitedly as she caught sight of X and the General. "Watch and take notes, mister! This is gonna be *so cool!*"

The Herc-Rhinos were nearly upon them. The turrets had barely made a dent in the fast-approaching swarm.

As usual, it fell to X and General Ishiro Tsujimori to dispose of the threat.

X flicked his wrists. With a click, a pair of narrow gray rectangles nearly as long as his torso shot from his sleeves into his hands. As he gripped them, they began to change, snapping and folding into the unmistakable shape of massive handguns. From the underside of the barrels, gleaming blades shot out to form deadly bayonets. From the base of each hilt were leather bands which ran back into the sleeves of his trench coat.

General Tsujimori removed and pocketed his purple rubber gloves. His exposed hands glowed bluish white from within, and the air around him crackled and hummed with electricity.

X took a few running steps and leapt into the air. Fire shot from the soles of his boots, launching him towards the swarm at speeds that would have killed a normal human. He dove and swerved to avoid the searing pink lasers streaming towards him, and his guns spoke a thunderous reply.

Three Herc-Rhinos flew past X, managing to land and cling to the hull, which meant it was the General's turn to act. With dramatic flair, he ran and drove one of his glowing fists towards the closest of the bugs. It was not a strong punch physically, and he pulled it at the last second to avoid shattering his bones, but the strength was not what mattered. As he made contact, a pulse of electricity surged from his body into the creature's, and arcs of pure white lightning engulfed it before it burst in a puff of acrid blue smoke.

As he dispatched of the second bug in similar fashion, the third bug figured out what was going on. Certain it had the element of surprise, it charged him from behind, hoping to impale him on its horn.

With a speed and grace that belied how old he looked, Tsujimori leapt straight up from a standing position and executed a graceful backflip over the charging Herc-Rhino's back. In midair, his hands reached down toward the insect and unleashed a furious storm of lightning bolts upon it. Those bolts that missed surged through the *Akira*'s hull and shot up through the insect's feet.

The creature bucked and flailed like a wild horse before bursting into another cloud of smoke.

Without missing a beat, Tsujimori landed hard on the ship, then swept his hands in front of him, creating a net of lightning bolts large enough to catch most of the approaching lasers like fish. He quickly drew his hands together and repelled the bolts back into the swarm.

Within the swarm, X was still blasting and slicing away at the attacking insects with his handheld cannons. He always aimed for the weak points in the bugs' armor or for their softer undersides, and despite the speed at which he darted about, he had yet to miss.

He barely had time to react as one of the bugs took a swipe at his face by bucking its head upward and catching him with its barbed horn.

It was a fascinatingly gruesome display. X reeled back, a thick spray of blood bursting from where his face had been. It was the blood, however, that was the strange part. Amongst the expected red trails were streams of creamy white and dark blue, and shredded mechanical objects which glinted silver in the ever-increasing sunlight.

The splatter suddenly froze in midair, then reversed itself, flowing back towards his body as if someone was playing a film reel backwards.

Just as suddenly as it had been erased, X's face had reappeared.

And it looked very angry.

X jabbed both bayonets into the offending bug's head and fired until its face was rendered as mangled as his had been. His regenerated face twisted into a wicked, vengeful smile as the beetle was slaughtered.

On the observation deck, Richard was awestruck.

As a reporter, he had a million questions about what he was seeing, but as a sane man, he just could not form the words to express them. All he was able to eventually stammer out was, "How... What *are* they?"

As had become her routine since meeting him, Nancy was there with a calm voice and a ready explanation. "You remember those Captain America comics from back in the day?" she asked.

"Yeah," Richard nodded, unsure of why she was bringing up comic books. Then again, the scene before him did look like a comic artist's dream rendered in three dimensions.

"It's kind of like that, except it's real. During the War, both the Allies and the Axis were engaged in genetic experiments, trying to make superhuman soldiers to lead their armies. You're looking at the only ones to have seen action on the battlefield and survived."

She pointed to the General, who was continuing to electrically pummel any bugs unfortunate enough to get close to or land on the ship. "General Ishiro Tsujimori of Japan, a human battery of sorts, capable of conducting, generating, and unleashing electrical energy to devastating effect."

She pointed to the swarm, where X continued to slaughter every bug he could see with his gun-swords. "Special Agent X of America, the world's only successful human cyborg, enhanced with regenerative abilities that effectively make him immortal."

Nancy glanced over at Chakra, and a mischievous grin snaked its way across her lips. "Even Chakra here was a test subject for Unit 731, and has powers of her own. Watch this." She turned to Hirata. "Captain, please do the honors."

Hirata whipped a loaded revolver from the holster at his side and aimed the barrel at Chakra's head.

Chakra was about to object, but the bullet that shattered her skull silenced her. Blood, brains, and bone fragments splattered across the windows, and her body slumped over the railing, completely lifeless.

Hirata returned his gun to its holster, his blank expression showing that he was completely unaffected by his heinous act. Nancy, too, remained calm and collected.

Richard, on the other hand, recoiled, his awe at the spectacle outside replaced by horror at the murder which had occurred right beside him. This is what finally pushed him over the edge into a panic. "What the-?" he shouted. "Good God!!! Why did-?"

"Give it a moment," Nancy said calmly as she patted him on the shoulder.

Chakra groaned as she stood back up, her head perfectly intact. There was no wound, no blood, indeed, no sign of any trauma at all. Aside from the offal which remained splattered across the windows, it was as if nothing had happened at all.

The dog-eared girl massaged the back of her head where the bullet had entered as if all that ailed her was a pounding headache. "Ow," she grumbled, more aggravated than hurt.

"See?" Nancy said. "She's completely fine. Nothing can kill her. Believe me, she's survived a lot. Chakra here was an attempt to turn a normal human into a yokai using science. It's really too bad all the research that went into her was lost, but that's how war goes sometimes."

"You could've just *told* him that!" Chakra snapped.

Nancy's calm demeanor did not break under Chakra's glare. "Consider that your punishment for abandoning your post again."

Chakra huffed loudly before turning back to continue watching the fight outside.

Richard blinked as he stared at Chakra, his mind forcing itself to accept what he had just witnessed. "So..." he began, then paused to organize his thoughts before continuing. "So the multi-colored blood, the lightning, the dog parts, all of that stuff was done to them in a lab?"

Nancy nodded. "Pretty much, yes." She laughed a little. "You know, it's kind of funny. There was a time when X and Ishiro would have been using their powers to try killing each other, but these days they have to work together."

Her voice became slightly grave as she continued. "You see, Richard, they're the only soldiers in the entire world who can do this job. They are the monsters protecting mankind from the monsters who want to destroy it."

General Tsujimori and X had managed to thin the swarm considerably, but a dozen Herc-Rhinos had still landed on the *Akira*, and were starting to claw their way through the fuselage. General Tsujimori knew it was time to pull out the big guns.

He knelt down, placing the palms of his hands flat against the hull, and began taking slow, deep breaths. He could sense the bugs starting to close in on him like prowling lions, but he did not move. Instead, he closed his eyes and focused only on breathing.

Then his whole body tensed.

The entire surface of the *Akira* flared with blinding blue-white light. Everything except the General was engulfed in lightning, and the bugs burst into brilliant multicolored flames.

The *Akira* gently rocked from side to side, just enough to allow gravity to pull the burning exoskeletons down into the water.

After a few seconds, the light faded, and the few Herc-Rhinos that remained in the air turned tail and fled.

The *Akira* ceased its rocking and resumed its journey, no worse for wear in the wake of the attack.

X landed beside the General, who staggered as he stood. Such huge bursts of energy were taxing for him, hence why he only used them as a last resort.

"You all right?" X said, a loud crack emanating from his shoulders as he rolled them. He offered an arm for support.

Tsujimori accepted the offer as he nodded. "I could use some tea."

They walked back to the elevator which had brought them there.

"I could've taken all of those ugly buggers by myself, you know," X said as the guns folded and retracted back into his sleeves.

Tsujimori shrugged as he smiled wryly at his fighting partner. "I would love to see you try, gaijin. You'd be begging for my help after two minutes."

CHAPTER 5

"To think," Ned Topol proclaimed as he stepped off the inflatable raft and onto the sandy shoreline, "we're the first people in history to set foot on the island of Rabu Nii!"

His companion, Jim Worth, dragged the raft onto the beach. "By which, you naturally mean the first *westerners*," he replied. "Don't forget, the natives on the neighboring islands have tales about this place."

Ned scoffed. "Myths, you mean."

The tropical island of Rabu Nii had only recently been discovered among the islands which collectively comprised Oceania. It had been rumored to exist for years, but had never been found on any official maps. Both Ned and Jim were part of an expedition funded by *Scientific Britannica* to explore it. Theirs was the first raft from the good ship *Delta* to reach the shore.

Jim took his camera from his knapsack and began snapping pictures of the coast and the dense green jungle, which rose up suddenly some fifty feet from the water. "You don't believe the stories? I thought folklorist was among the many credentials you like bragging about."

Ned shrugged. "Do I think some natives wound up here for one reason or another? Sure. Why not?" He checked his compass, more out of habit than for any real practical reason. "Do I think their greatest heroes came here to fight dragons as some coming-of-age ritual? Heck no. Dragons aren't real."

"What about the ones on Komodo?" Jim smirked.

"Those aren't literal dragons, and you know it!" Ned fired back playfully. Jim always nitpicked his words like that. It was a habit which went back to their university days. "Getting back to the battle of semantics, fine, I'll correct myself. We're the first *westerners* to set foot here." He glanced back in the *Delta*'s direction. The second inflatable raft, which carried both the interns and the equipment, was still floating about halfway between the ship and the shore. "What do you think the holdup is? I thought they were right behind us."

Jim smiled. "Probably Barbara getting seasick again. Remember how often she tossed her cookies on the way here?"

The pair shared a laugh at the intern's misfortune which was interrupted by a thunderous **BOOM!** from the jungle that shook the ground, knocking them over.

While Jim let out a string of startled exclamations and shocked quandaries as to what had just happened, Ned's attention was drawn back to the water.

The second raft was gone.

Had it sunk? No, that made no sense. It was an inflatable raft, and it had been intact just a moment ago. He had never heard of an inflatable raft just sinking like a stone, and even if it had, where were the occupants and equipment? They were close enough to shore that the water was not especially deep, so they should have been visible.

Any other thoughts were pushed aside when he saw a massive black hump break the surface where the raft had been, visible only for a moment before vanishing underwater again, causing hardly so much as a ripple as it went.

He rubbed his eyes as confusion set in. He tried to figure out what he had just seen. Was it a dolphin? He dismissed the thought immediately. Too big, wrong color, and no dorsal fin. An orca, perhaps? Again, no fin, not to mention that orcas were not native to these waters.

The hump resurfaced, farther away, moving towards the *Delta*.

"Jim," he said, tapping the photographer on the shoulder. "Point that camera of yours at the water. There's something crazy out there."

"Can't be any crazier than what I'm seeing."

The awestruck quiver in Jim's brief reply spoke volumes. Ned turned, and was rendered silent by a vision of dinosaurs.

He blinked his eyes, but this changed nothing. The dinosaurs were still there.

Well, they were *like* dinosaurs, at least. Despite his many credentials, dinosaurs had never been his speciality, but these creatures had the right features for him to identify some of the species before him. Triceratops, Stegosaurus, T-rex, Raptor…and that was as far as his knowledge extended. He did not recognize any of the others from any books or movies he had seen in the past.

Come to think of it, he barely even recognized the ones he *could* identify. They were bigger than he expected, probably bigger than most scientists would say was accurate, and the details looked all wrong in ways he could not quite put his finger on.

Strangest of all was how the creatures encircled them as they marched from the jungle to the beach. It made no sense. This group before him appeared to be a mix of carnivores and herbivores, which would make them natural enemies. They should have been fighting amongst themselves, but they moved as one collective pack as they stalked from the jungle to the beach.

In fact, their collective attention was focused on Ned and Jim.

Ned gulped nervously. The way the dinosaurs were glaring at him and Jim put him on edge. Their eyes conveyed menace, something far more intense than hunting or territorialism, and the sentiment chilled his heart.

He fought the urge to wipe the sweat from his eyes lest a sudden movement spook the creatures into attacking. "Those are…" Disbelief stopped the words in his throat, but he forced them out. "Those are dinosaurs…"

"No kidding…" Jim said, his voice conveying an equal sense of disbelief.

"What should we do?" Ned whispered as he blinked his eyes dry of sweat.

"What makes you think *I* know how to act around a bunch of bloody dinosaurs?" Jim snapped back. He was clearly trying not to panic, but he was just barely succeeding in that regard.

Ned tried not to take the sharp reply personally, but terrified urgency colored his tone as well. "They're animals, right? You've photographed dangerous animals before. So what did you do when things got like…well, like this?" He glanced at the camera. "Would a flash from that thing spook them?"

"It might. Or it might just tick them off."

"Well, give me *something* to work with!"

Jim tried to think, which proved difficult while staring at animals that should have been extinct. "First of all, no sudden movements."

"Really? No fooling?" Ned snapped sarcastically in his fear.

Jim sighed furiously, but chose to let it go. "Back slowly towards the raft with me. They might recognize our intent to leave."

An image of the mysterious black hump flashed through Ned's mind. "I'm not sure the water is much safer, Jim."

"That's where the *Delta* is."

"Point taken."

Moving together, Ned and Jim slowly backed towards the raft, but only got two steps before a new creature froze them in place once more.

The latest beast to arrive towered over the trees like a Titan from Greek mythology, standing in a slightly-hunched but still upright stance. In the most general sense, the beast looked like a Tyrannosaurus, or maybe an Allosaurus. It was a theropod dinosaur of some sort, but a hundred times bigger than anything in the museums or on the beach. Its light brown skin was rough like alligator hide. Its arms were long enough to appear useful, but were still small compared to the rest of it, and the hands each had two fingers and an opposable thumb. A shimmering ivory horn jutted from the snout, its ruddy tip indicating it as a weapon that saw a lot of use in battle.

The behemoth scrutinized the humans with intelligent eyes, its low growl vibrating through the air to still the beating of their hearts.

"We're screwed," Ned whimpered.

"Maybe not," replied Jim, although he was not sure he believed it himself. "Animals only attack when threatened. We've done nothing to provoke them."

Ned stared into the towering monster's eyes, and saw an emotion he had seen before, though mostly in horror movies, and never from a reptile.

It was hatred. Pure, unfettered hatred.

The enormous monster roared. It was a piercing, malevolent sound, and though it might have been his imagination, to Ned's ears, it held authority, like a wordless command.

The dinosaurs on the beach charged.

No point in being cautious now.

He ran.

A scream drew Ned's attention, and he turned to see Jim impaled on the tail spikes of a Stegosaurus. He did not see what happened after that. In all certainty, Jim was dead. Ned's focus was to save himself now.

Getting the raft in the water would slow him down, and his glance back at Jim had revealed a raptor was closing in on him fast. His only hope was something he was not even sure would work. He remembered reading somewhere that most dinosaurs could not swim, and thus avoided entering the water. Of course, it was just a theory. Before today, no scientist had ever seen a living dinosaur or how it reacted to water.

If ever there was a time to test this idea, it was now.

Exerting as much energy as he could, he charged past the raft and continued right into the water, switching clumsily from running to swimming when he stumbled a few feet out.

Ned heard roaring behind him, but it did not sound like it was drawing any closer to him.

Despite the risk, he paused and looked back to the shore.

All of the dinosaurs had stopped at the water's edge, snarling, roaring, and snapping their jaws at him as if they were scolding him for not playing fair.

Thrilled by both his victory and the adrenaline pumping through his veins, Ned laughed triumphantly. "Suckers!" he shouted. "What's wrong, you bunch of cowards? Scared of a little water? Too delicate to get your feet wet?" He splashed water at them. "No wonder you sorry geckos went extinct!"

The roaring grew louder and angrier, almost as if the dinosaurs had understood his insult. Part of Ned thought that was impossible, but a few minutes ago, he thought an island where dinosaurs still lived was equally impossible.

So many thoughts were sailing through his mind as he floated in the water. He had survived, but Jim was dead. Nobody would believe him, unless someone on the *Delta* had seen what had happened. How would he even get back to the *Delta*? He was not sure he could swim the distance, and he could not use the raft until the beach was clear of danger.

He refocused his attention on the largest of the beasts, whom he now believed was the dinosaurs' leader. Given how big it was, there was nothing to stop it from wading out and scooping him up in its jaws, yet it had not moved so much as an inch toward him.

He realized the giant's expression had changed. Ned was not used to seeing emotions on reptilian faces, so it took a moment to figure out what it was.

Smugness?

The creaking of metal drew Ned's attention to the ship, and his heart sank.

Something that looked like a massive snake was wrapping itself around the *Delta*, the sinewy coils crushing it the way a python crushes its prey. Behind it, some impossibly large beast covered in smooth silver scales rose from the waves. It might have been a barracuda, based on the head, but it had arms like some kind of dragon.

Then the black hump reappeared in front of him, followed by a spray of water and a flash of white daggers.

CHAPTER 6

"That. Was. AMAZING!!!" Richard shouted when he saw X and the General, unable to contain his stunned excitement. Despite his desire to remain professional, he could not deny the thrill surging through him in the wake of the battle he had just witnessed.

Nancy had led him from the observation deck to the secure elevator to greet the supermen who had defeated the swarm. In the time it had taken to get there, Richard had become more and more amazed by what he had seen. His excitement was surpassed only by that of Chakra, who had immediately clung like a bur to X's sleeve the moment she saw him, much to his mild embarrassment.

"You two killed those bugs like...well, like bugs!" he continued. "The lightning, and the flying through the air with the guns... I- I've never seen any human being do stuff like that before!"

"Then you haven't been paying very close attention to your surroundings," General Tsujimori replied, his tone as casual as if he were a white collar man come home from working at the factory.

"I need details!" Richard held out the recording stick like a microphone. "What's it like to use your powers? How do they work? Is there-?"

"Incoming transmission," said a mechanical voice on the intercom. "Source: Groom Lake. Message Level: Priority One."

"Oh, great," X sighed angrily.

His misery was echoed by the General. In fact, everyone except Richard seemed irritated to hear the announcement.

The super soldiers left for the conference room. Chakra had released X's arm immediately, knowing better than to cling when such a call came through. She slumped against the wall, grumbling something about the mood being killed before slinking away. Captain Catigiri left in the opposite direction of his superiors.

"Why's everyone so glum all of a sudden?" Richard asked.

Nancy began walking down the hall, motioning for Richard to follow. "Only one person ever calls from Groom Lake these days, and that's Michael Sun, our official liaison between the Red Dragons and the US government."

"What the heck is Groom Lake?"

Nancy's eyes went wide as she stopped dead in her tracks, like someone who had arrived at a fancy vacation spot only to remember she had left the oven on at home. "Oh shoot!" she quietly exclaimed to herself. It took her a moment to formulate an answer. "Um… I'm afraid that's one of the few things I can't tell you, Richard." She smiled apologetically. "Let's just say Uncle Sam wants it kept secret. For now, anyway. So please just forget you heard that, all right? Trust me, it's not a door you want to open."

Richard's instincts told him that there was actually one heck of a juicy story connected to this Groom Lake, whatever it was, but Nancy's tone and expression told him that it would have to wait. He silently filed the name away, and turned his line of questioning back to more immediate subjects. "Okay, how about this, then. You still haven't told me what this Red Dragon organization is all about, beyond killing giant bugs, that is."

"I haven't? Really?" Nancy thought back over what she had told Richard thus far, and realized that, indeed, she had not told him. "Well darn, I guess you're right. Let's fix that, then. You change out of your PJs and we'll get some breakfast-to-go in the cafeteria."

"To go? Why?"

"Because the archival footage isn't in the cafeteria."

"So *nobody* saw the fight?" Michael Sun asked, his stern glare flickering on one of the many screens within the private conference room.

General Tsujimori pinched the bridge of his nose as if he were getting a headache, which, given the conversation, he was on the cusp of. "For the hundredth time, *no,* Michael-san. We're the only ship for miles around."

"You checked?"

"If there were any other ships nearby, the bugs got to them first. We received no distress calls, and got no radar contacts before the bugs showed up. Believe me, no one saw anything they weren't meant to."

X crossed his arms over his chest. "There's something else you're calling about, isn't there, Mike?"

"What else could it possibly be?" Michael leaned back in his chair, his unmistakably accusatory gaze unwavering. "We keep secrets from the public, not each other." His eyebrows arched towards the heavens. "Right?"

A faint red glare shimmered in X's glowing eyes as they narrowed. "I don't especially like your tone today, Mike."

Michael's voice was very sharp as he responded. "So what? Operation Red Dragon is a secret clandestine organization the public doesn't know about, and we all want it to stay that way, don't we?" He tapped his finger on his desk. "You two would never do anything to *compromise* that secrecy, would you?"

X's reply was even sharper in tone. "I also don't appreciate what you're implying."

"My job is to make sure this conspiracy *stays* a conspiracy, X, and I take my job very seriously, unlike you freaks gallivanting around the world playing superhero. Don't forget, while you're off globetrotting on that giant cigar case you call a ship, *I'm* back here on the mainland with politicians breathing down my neck, expecting solid reasons to not step in and run this group the way *they* want to run it."

"Is there *anything* else?" Tsujimori asked, desperate to end the conversation. "Because there had *really* better be something else."

Michael shot X a final dirty look before answering. "I need an update on where the big ones are."

The General nodded. "What a coincidence, so do we."

Michael stared at Tsujimori in stunned silence for a moment before shouting, "You *lost* them? How do you lose something as big as they are?"

The General shrugged. He had no answer, not even a snarky one.

"Darn it all, find them!" Michael snapped. "I don't care if you have to drain the whole blasted ocean to do it! Find them before they show up on the mainland!"

With that, the transmission cut out.

General Tsujimori and X exited the conference room. "How do you read that?" the General asked.

"He knows," X replied. "Somebody tipped him off about Mr. Godfrey."

"I thought the same. The question is: Who was it?"

"Could be anyone."

Awkward silence hung in the air. General Tsujimori could feel X's eyes glaring at him. "Don't look at me," he said. "Frankly, I'm offended you would even consider that as a possibility. We concocted this plan together, after all."

X adjusted the collar on his coat. "Of the two of us, Ishiro, I'm not the one who committed mutiny during the War."

Tsujimori's eyes narrowed until they were practically slits. "Well, of the two of us, I'm not the one who wiped an entire island of innocents off the map."

"My actions were *justified.*"

"So were *mine.*"

They stared each other down for a full minute, saying nothing.

"All right, we're both clear," X finally said. "Who else do we put on the watch list?"

Tsujimori tapped his chin in thought. "Those rooms are the only places where anyone can make a call to Groom Lake, or anywhere without being seen or heard, and there are only two others on this ship who can get past the card reader."

"Nancy and Hirata," X nodded. "Can't be both of them. We'd have noticed if they were working together. Changes in behavior, making excuses for unexplained absences... It's got to be either one or the other."

"Captain Catigiri has served me faithfully since his recruitment," the General said. "He is no traitor. I trust the man with my life."

"Personally, I don't fully trust anyone who doesn't talk," X replied. "Besides, I know where Miss Boardwalk's allegiance lies. I hand-picked her for this job."

"It could also be Chakra. She has easy access to everything of yours." Tsujimori shot X an accusatory look. "*Very* easy."

X reacted strongly, shoving his gloved finger in the General's face. "It's *not* her!"

"How can you be so certain? She regularly abandons her duties, not to mention the way she acts around you is just unnatural. She hangs on you like lights on a Christmas tree."

"You were married once, Ishiro, just like me. You know what that bond is like. I saw the way you and Saeko used to look at each other. Would she have betrayed you?"

Tsujimori averted his gaze, his head hanging low as memories of his late wife flooded his mind. As a soldier, he was trained to control his emotions, but this topic always affected him.

God, he missed her.

X picked up on his partner's growing sadness. "Not that it matters," he said quietly, realizing he had crossed a line. He offered no consolation, mostly because he was not good at it.

"I'll concede...that Chakra's the least likely suspect," Tsujimori said as he steadied his spirit. "Until we have more evidence, though, I will not rule her out."

X nodded. "Fair enough, I guess. But I know it's not her."

"For your sake, gaijin, I hope you're right. Losing a spouse for any reason is a pain I wish on no one."

A young cadet, fresh out of the academy as of the previous month, approached the pair. A look of concern adorned his face. "There you are, sirs!" he said. "We have some new activity."

The discussion of treachery was tabled, and both men snapped back into action mode. "Activity where?" the General asked.

"We have three potential incidents. First, contact with a research vessel was lost in the vicinity of Rabu Nii. Its name was the *Delta*, I believe."

"What?!?" snapped X. "The Navy's supposed to have ships there specifically to prevent that sort of thing!"

"No clue how they got past the blockade, sir. Must've been dumb luck."

"Blast! What else?"

"Seismic activity outside of Fukuoka is increasing, with the epicenter moving towards the city. Lastly, we detected another swarm of bugs moving towards the town of Boca de Vacca on the coast of Chile."

The General's brow furrowed. "Where the Pterosaur nests are."

X cracked his knuckles as he mentally organized the incidents in order of importance, then he spoke. "We're heading for Fukuoka anyway, so we maintain that course and stick to our mission. I'll put in a request for CIGOR to check out Rabu Nii."

With that, he and the General departed, each heading in opposite directions to prepare themselves for the tasks ahead.

The cadet stood in place, his head darting back and forth between his superiors in befuddlement. "Um... Sirs?" he asked. "What about the swarm heading for Chile? Shouldn't we do something about that?"

"They'll be fine!" the General called back.

The cadet's befuddlement increased. "With all due respect, Sirs, that town has no defense against the bugs!"

"They have the best defense in the world!" X called back.

"But the secrecy!"

"It can't last forever!"

In 1962, a Russian nuclear submarine had disappeared somewhere off the coast of Japan. The incident had initially been a major point of Cold War contention, with Russia blaming America for attacking and sinking the vessel. For three long months, it looked like this event would be the spark that started World War Three. As it turned out, no evidence was ever found of an attack, and the tension had subsided. The sub was simply declared lost at sea after the investigation was closed, though suspicion of sabotage or a covert act of war remained popular amongst Russian citizens and Soviet officials itching for conflict.

The truth was far less scandalous than the rumors. The submarine had merely sunk due to a freak malfunction in its systems. It was an unfortunate accident, nothing more.

Only one creature on Earth knew where the lost vessel was, and he had gone to its resting place to feed.

Though he knew where it was, he had played no part in the submarine's fate. He normally did not bother attacking human vessels unless they were stupid enough to attack him first – indeed, he had spent much of his time in the sea saving human vessels from other attackers – but he was a creature that needed energy as much as food to survive, and even two years after the event, the ship's reactor still had plenty to give him.

This energy had been strange to him when he had first sensed it years ago. It was like fire, and yet at the same time, nothing like fire. It was a primal thing that Earth had not seen in eons, only this type was unnatural. He had no specific name for it, but he knew that the humans made it, and it could make him stronger.

He clenched the reactor in his razor-sharp teeth, floating motionless far beneath the waves as the energy flowed into his body, warming his core. His horns flickered with faint light from within.

He was going to need all the energy he could get in the days to come. So would the others.

Victory over their foes depended on it.

Even suspended in the water so many miles away, he felt the tremors on the land as the dinosaurs made their way towards the cities.

He knew that was where he would go next.

CHAPTER 7

The silent black-and-white image being projected on the screen was one familiar to Richard, as it would be to anyone who viewed it: D-Day, the Battle of Normandy, though presented with greater clarity than Richard had ever seen it before.

He was seated in a darkened room arranged like a very small movie theater, watching the footage play before him on a ten-foot screen while he dined on a breakfast of scrambled eggs and toast. Nancy, who had quickly downed a few strips of bacon on the way over, sat on his left, and provided a running commentary for what he was seeing.

"Newton's Third Law of Thermodynamics states that for every action, there is an equal and opposite reaction," she said. "Most people don't think about it all that much, but this applies to more than just physics. In fact, human actions can invoke very strange reactions from the environment. The World Wars in particular were especially harsh. You ever notice how heavily edited the footage from D-Day is whenever it's shown on TV?"

Richard nodded.

"Well," Nancy continued, "you're about to see why."

The view of the battlefield panned quickly, pointing towards the ridge where the German artillery lay just in time to see them explode. It was not from a bomb, though. Even through the occasional grain of the film and jostling of the camera, Richard could tell that the ground had blown apart from below the surface. Through the debris, he could see a large, snub-nosed reptilian head on the end of a long neck snaking outward.

For a few seconds, the scene was nothing but a blurry mess as the cameraman ran for safety. Once he was settled behind one of the many obstacles on the beach, he pointed his camera back at the lumbering behemoth.

Indeed, behemoth was an accurate description. Richard had heard theories that the references to a creature called behemoth in the Bible, specifically the Book of Job, were describing a sauropod dinosaur, and this creature which had been captured on film fit that description to a T. Legs like an oak, tail like a cedar.

The beast paid little heed to the soldiers under its feet. In fact, it looked like a spooked animal which had been rudely awoken and was fleeing for safety.

Richard was amazed at the sight, but Nancy continued speaking in her casual tone as if it were nothing new to her. She had seen this film many times before. "Random incidents like this were how it started," she said. "In fact, the First World War was what brought the small ones out in the first place. You know how the first contemporary sightings of the Loch Ness Monster were in the Thirties?"

"Of course," Richard said.

"That's because all the commotion in Europe disturbed the creatures who were dormant in the lake. But the second war gave us the atomic bomb, and that's when all hell *really* broke loose."

Nancy delivered a quick hand signal to the projection booth behind them, and the reel switched to newer-looking footage, a home movie filmed on super-8 from the look of it. It depicted a suburban American family going on a picnic out in the desert, having a grand old time before the ants ruined it.

Ants the length of boxcars.

"Our action was to split the atom and make a weapon out of it," Nancy continued. "Earth's reaction was the Kaiju."

"The what?"

"Kaiju. It's Japanese for 'strange beast', so we use it as the catchall term for any large, unusual creature who shows up. Those ants are Kaiju, as was the Brontosaurus earlier, and as is this bird."

With another signal from Nancy, the reel switched again, revealing footage of an Air Force jet suddenly finding its wing shorn off by what looked like a hawk which was every bit its equal in size. The bird clung to the jet as it spiraled, but released it and flew away before it crashed. It was hard to tell if the pilot had managed to eject or not.

Richard set his plate on the floor, too enraptured with the footage for any of his attention to be diverted to eating. "So, you mentioned the A-bomb earlier. Are these things new mutations caused by nuclear tests, or are they prehistoric creatures that were hidden until we woke them up with the bomb?"

"Very good question," Nancy said. "The answer is yes."

Another signal, and the reel switched again, this time to a place that looked like the Savanah. The footage of a tyrannosaurus-like beast graphically killing and devouring a hippopotamus made Richard glad he had stopped eating.

"The mutations mostly do their own thing. Unless they're provoked, rabid, or somehow developed a taste for us, they avoid humans just like normal animals do. The prehistoric ones – those are the dinos and the bugs – are the primary concern for our operation."

Signal. Reel switch. Silent footage of X and General Tsujimori engaging a horde of dinosaurs on the ground now played on the screen.

"It turns out that resistance to change isn't a trait exclusive to mankind. The ancient Kaiju don't like the fact that they aren't the rulers of Earth anymore, and ever since they resurfaced, they've been eager to wipe humanity off the map. That's where we come in. Operation Red Dragon is an international paramilitary unit forged during World War Two, tasked with keeping the Kaiju under control and, more importantly, hidden from the public by preventing them from getting to any major cities. To that end, we have X and General Ishiro Tsujimori, two veteran super soldiers who excel at killing Kaiju."

The image vanished as the reel ran out, and the lights came on.

"Lucky for us, most atomic tests are done in isolated areas, like deserts and islands in the Pacific, far from any major cities and high-traffic areas. So it's been easy to keep most of the Kaiju in line all these years."

Richard scratched his head. "If your job is to keep all of this hidden, you've done a terrible job. Reports of sightings get out all the time. Trust me, I would know. I've spoken to the witnesses myself and reported their accounts in some pretty big news outlets."

Nancy folded her arms. "Indeed you have. And how many of those reports are taken seriously, if I may ask?"

Richard had no answer for that.

"Exactly," she continued. "The best way to keep a secret is to convince everyone that it's a lie, then it keeps itself. That was the whole point of things like Project Blue Book. We got a few reputable guys in lab coats to say that something is impossible, and the problem was solved. Of course, we didn't expect Hyneck to change his tune so easily..."

"Why keep it a secret at all?" Richard interrupted. "What about all the stuff we could learn by studying these things?" Richard pointed at the screen, even though it was blank. "What if the mutations could help us find a cure for radiation poisoning? And imagine the ramifications studying those dinosaurs would have on paleontology! The real things look nothing like the paintings and models in museums!"

"Give the paleontologists a break, Richard. You can only get so much from a few bone fragments."

"Point taken. My question still stands unanswered."

Nancy stood and headed for the exit. Richard grabbed his plate and followed as she replied. "There is a philosophy behind it. I don't necessarily agree with it myself, but it's what's kept the conspiracy going all these years. See, Richard, we're in the middle of a Cold War.

Two superpowers armed to the teeth with world-destroying weapons are each trying to prove that *they're* the ones in control, and they each have their respective citizens convinced that they are." They dropped their breakfast plates off on a rolling rack by the kitchen. "It's an illusion, sure, but it's kept the world spinning. So long as Capitalism and Communism are run by rational human beings, neither side will want to be the first to cross the line and bring on the apocalypse. The powers that be believe the Kaiju would break that illusion of control, not just for nations, but for mankind itself. The moment Kaiju pass from easily dismissed pseudoscience into undeniable reality, mankind will panic, because it will no longer be the pinnacle of creation, and it'll give the world governments an excuse to finally launch those nukes they've been stockpiling." She shrugged. "Like I said, I don't entirely agree with that, but I'm also in no position to argue with it just yet."

"I don't know if I agree with it either," Richard said. "Sure, people would be scared, but you guys can kill the Kaiju. I've seen that with my own eyes."

"We can kill the small ones. The big ones are another matter."

"Big ones?"

The intercom buzzed to life. "Coastal perimeter reached. All personnel heading for the mainland, please proceed to the main hangar."

"Time enough to explain that later," Nancy said in response to Richard's question. "Right now, there's someone on the mainland I think you'll want to meet."

CHAPTER 8

X was under no illusions about the fact that he was not a normal human being. The experiment which made him a cyborg had seen to that. He was capable of things no other man on Earth could do. During the war, he had been a one-man army serving the Stars and Stripes with his built-in gadgetry and enhanced biology. He had fought in both the Atlantic and Pacific theaters, and the Axis had learned quickly to fear him. Even the letter that served as his name had struck fear into their hearts. Some Nazis had been executed as traitors for refusing to wear swastikas because the shape reminded them of him. That had helped thin their numbers quite a bit.

If anyone on God's Green Earth had the potential to let his ego run rampant, it would have been X. With his unparalleled power and rugged determination, he could start a revolution and crown himself immortal king of the world if he wanted to.

Of course, he would never do such a thing. For starters, X had no interest in politics. He was a man of action, born and bred to lead soldiers on the battlefield, not bureaucrats in an office. He was also a man of faith. He may have known how extraordinary he was, but he would never call himself a god.

Especially not when an actual god was living on the ship.

He stood in front of two massive doors, the largest ones on the *Akira*, behind which resided one of the creatures that could instill humility in the most arrogant of men. He screwed up his courage. Behind these doors resided CIGOR, and it was X's job to request his services. The same technology that made him a cyborg had been used to bring CIGOR back to full health, so they shared a bond of sorts. CIGOR, however, was not a beast to be commanded like some household pet. He sided with the Red Dragons only because he chose to. Living aboard the *Akira* was beneficial to both CIGOR and the crew, but he had the right to say no to any request whenever he wanted, for whatever reason, or for no reason at all. If he did, there was nothing anyone on the ship could do about it.

The doors opened slowly, revealing complete blackness within. A blue light blinked on, hovering far above X's tall frame. The light faintly reflected off of something smooth and silver right in front of it, but otherwise did little to illuminate the room.

The light narrowed like a scrutinizing eye at X, and a metallic chittering echoed from the room down the corridor like the call of a mechanical bird. X relaxed slightly. He knew CIGOR's sounds and mannerisms well from years of service together, and this was not a threatening sound.

"Good morning, CIGOR," he said, bowing as he might have done before a king.

CIGOR responded with several short chirps akin to an arrangement of notes played in the middle range of a pipe organ. X recognized it as a question, asking where they were.

"We're just outside of Japanese waters, about to meet with the Doctor. I..." X's body tensed up, and he paused to clear his throat, not because it actually needed clearing, but because he needed to collect his thoughts again, lest his hardened exterior crack. "I would like you to check something out for us."

Another inquisitive chirp, pitched down.

"A research ship went missing at Rabu Nii. The *Delta*."

Tittering, then a brief squawk.

"That's what we suspect. Unfortunately, we have to be here, or we'd go look for survivors ourselves. I was hoping..." He took a breath to steady his nerves. The longer X stood in CIGOR's presence, the smaller he felt. "...to ask if you might look for us."

Silence hung in the air for a moment as the blue light of CIGOR's eye stared unblinking at the black-clad human.

CIGOR made a noise that sounded like a shriek.

X bowed respectfully. "Thank you."

In the hallway ahead of him and Nancy, Richard saw X leave an adjacent corridor and turn to walk towards the hangar. They fell in pace behind him. Apparently, wherever Richard and Nancy were going in the shuttle, X would be going as well.

As he passed the corridor, Richard casually glanced down it, not really expecting to see anything unusual, only to stop dead in his tracks.

He did not really know what he was looking at, because whatever it was remained in the shadows behind massive, slowly closing doors. All he could see clearly was a blue light, but he swore it looked more like an eye than a lightbulb.

Just before the doors shut, this glowing blue eye stared right at him, its cold gaze piercing straight through him to freeze his very soul.

Once the doors were shut, Richard saw an arrangement of letters nearly as tall as the doors themselves painted on them. They were all capitals, and spelled a word he had never seen or heard before: CIGOR.

He blinked, feeling chilled to the core without really knowing why.

"What the...?" he whispered to himself as he stood rooted in place, eyes affixed to the mysterious doors.

He jumped when Nancy tugged on his sleeve.

"Hey," she said. "You coming?"

His eyes did not want to waver from the doors. "Yeah, but..." He struggled to find the words. "I just saw ..." He raised his finger and pointed down the corridor. "What's down there?"

Nancy glanced down the corridor. "Well..." She thought, then shook her head as if discouraging herself from speaking. "Something too complicated to explain right now. Come on. We've got places to be."

The shuttle took its occupants from the *Akira* to the countryside just beyond Fukuoka, a city in Northern Japan whose name made most immature English speakers snicker when they saw it written out.

After all of the strangeness he had been subjected to over the past few hours, Richard was surprised to find the shuttle descending towards something a bit more mundane: a pillbox, the kind of simple cement fortress he knew the Japanese had built on island outposts during the War. It was in the middle of a clearing, the unnatural flatness of which initially scratched at his brain before he realized how similar it was to the one from which he had departed America. Though familiar, it was still out of place, at least to him. As far as he knew, pillboxes had not been built on the Japanese mainland during the War. As they drew closer, he could see that the concrete did not appear to be terribly weathered, meaning it must have been a more recent construction. The pillbox and its clearing sat in the middle of a vast sea of trees which gradually turned to distant mountains in the west.

The shuttle flew and landed without concern for being seen, for there were no roads or hiking trails for miles around. Once they had settled on the ground, Richard suddenly felt slightly dizzy. It was a sensation he had felt before. A few years ago, he had taken a trip to the east coast of America just in time to experience a very small freak earthquake. There had been several states separating him and the epicenter, so he only felt the tail end of the shockwaves, but those subtle vibrations had made him feel imbalanced in similar fashion to how he felt now.

Knowing that the Red Dragons went wherever Kaiju might attack, he was fairly certain the vibrations he currently felt had nothing to do with the shifting of tectonic plates.

Richard rose uneasily, expecting to disembark and eventually be brought to yet another strange new location, but Nancy stopped him by putting a hand on his shoulder. "No, not this time," she said as she guided him back down to his seat. "Only those with superpowers get off at this stop. You'll be watching from here."

"Where it's safe?" Richard asked.

Nancy shrugged. "Well, saf_er_, at least. Besides, we're picking someone up who wants to meet you."

The shuttle remained grounded for three minutes, during which time General Tsujimori and X disembarked. As he waited, Richard focused his attention on the view outside his small round window, looking for any sign of Kaiju in the clearing or surrounding forest. He saw nothing obvious, and so it remained as they took off again, rising about one hundred feet into the air. He was certain that he must have been missing something, so he remained focused on the view outside, looking for even the smallest hint of anything unnatural. He was only vaguely aware of the footsteps that came up behind his chair.

"So, this is the one then?" said a smooth, stoic voice from straight out of Richard's past. It was a voice he had only ever heard once before, but it had burrowed its way deep into his memory. It had spoken words that influenced the course of his entire life.

It was the voice of Absurdity itself.

He rose, turned, and could not believe his eyes.

Standing before him, looking exactly as he had when he spoke at the university twelve years ago, was Dr. Daisuke Armitage.

Left behind *again.*

Chakra could not quite decide how she felt about this treatment of X constantly leaving her on the bridge of the *Akira* while he and enemy-turned-ally the General went off to fight monsters.

On the one hand, she knew it was because he wanted to protect her, and it was very sweet and chivalrous of him. Honestly, she did not really hate this treatment. X had always been protective of her since the day they met. It had been like a scene from a storybook, X swooping in like a dashing knight to save her from the lab where she had been experimented on during the War. After all the tortures that came with being a human guinea pig, being put through horrific procedures that had turned her into something most people would shun as an inhuman freak, being cared for to the point of coddling by someone who only had her best interests at heart was not the worst way to live. Indeed, some women would kill for such luxury.

But darn it all, she was immortal! Even if she was killed in a fight, she would come back. She always did. Those scientists had turned her into an impossible-to-kill soldier with enhanced canine senses, and even if she specifically was never meant to see combat – she was a woman, after all – she hated to think that she had endured the horrors of those bizarre experiments only for her powers to go to waste as she sat on her butt.

There was no reason for her to not be part of the action, but no, she was still on the ship with the bridge crew, assigned the soul-sucking task of staring at a radar screen while her husband was off having all of the fun.

Yes, she enjoyed the coddling, but she would have enjoyed fighting alongside X even more. She felt that it would just deepen their already strong bond. After all, weren't couples supposed to do things together?

It was especially unfair since the reporter *did* get to go with them. No powers, no training, and no clue what was going on, yet he was there and she was here. Sure, she understood the plan which required him to go where the action was, but that did not mean she had to like it.

A blip on the radar disrupted her stewing. The signal was soon joined by others, and registered blue, indicating aquatic Kaiju. They moved quickly, sailing right under the *Akira* without stopping. This was not uncommon; the aquatic ones rarely attacked flying targets. Too much work for no guaranteed payoff.

Chakra noted their trajectory. They were heading for the mainland.

In fact, they were heading straight for the city of Fukuoka.

"Uh-oh," she said aloud, more to herself than anyone else. They had expected trouble to come by land, but not by sea. X and the others would be caught by surprise.

Unless…

Chakra transmitted a warning signal to the outpost, then slipped away from her post yet again when she was sure no one else on the bridge was looking. Stealthily but quickly, she made her way towards the hangar.

Jenny, who sat nearby at CIGOR's monitoring console, sensed that the dog-eared girl had left again, and with an aggravated sigh, diverted some of her attention to the radar.

She did not see the blue targets, which had already vanished from the screen.

All she saw was an enormous red signature moving towards the mainland in hot pursuit.

Radar was not Jenny's specialty, but everyone who was part of Operation Red Dragon knew what a massive red target meant. Her mouth went dry in shock as she transmitted a second warning.

"It's you," Richard whispered, awestruck. "You… I… Um…"

He sat back down, trying to collect his thoughts and formulate them into something intelligible. This was amazing. Here he was, Doctor Daisuke Armitage, the man who had given him a purpose in life. Armitage was Richard's idol. There had been a time following the college lecture when Richard had tried tracking the doctor down, but he had eventually given up, for Armitage had proven impossible to find.

Yet here he was, onboard the futuristic ship that belonged to a top secret organization which hunted giant monsters, none of which Richard, despite researching such things his whole life, had encountered himself before yesterday.

He had dreamed of one day speaking to Armitage, and now that he had the chance, he was stammering like an idiot.

"Take your time, young Richard," Armitage said.

Richard blinked in astonishment. "You know my name?" He shook his head, mentally chastising himself for sounding like a star-struck schoolgirl. "Well, of course you would know. They, uh, they probably told you, right? The Red Dragon people, I mean." Another mental scolding. Red Dragon people? No one talks like that.

Armitage sat down across from Richard. "Actually, I know you from your articles. I also remember seeing you in the crowd in Fifty-two when I spoke at your college."

Richard might as well have been told that he had inherited all of the gold in Fort Knox tax-free. He was speechless.

"I'm quite impressed with your work," Armitage continued. "In fact, I'm the one who recommended you for this little gambit."

Richard's head swam with a million questions. How had Armitage known about him? Why recommend *him*, of all people? What gambit was he talking about? How deeply involved was he with these people?

Before he could formulate any of these questions into coherent words, the distinct roar of rockets flared outside his window, drawing his attention back outside.

It was X. He was flying at top speed back the way they had come, towards the city.

Richard felt the hairs on his arm stand up as static electricity filled the air, then he was shocked to see General Tsujimori march through the cabin towards the cockpit, a mixed look of anger, determination, and panic on his face.

Richard rubbed his eyes in disbelief. He was certain the General had been on the ground when the shuttle took off. How had he gotten back onboard while the ship was still airborne?

"Something's wrong," Nancy said, her voice filled with concern for the first time since Richard had met her. "Something's very, very wrong."

The ship jerked around sharply and followed X, not bothering to ascend beyond its current altitude as it zoomed towards Fukuoka.

Nancy was right. Something had to be wrong. They were guaranteed to be seen if they got too close to the city.

If Richard had to guess, the growing sense of urgency he felt aboard the ship meant that remaining hidden was not currently a priority.

In which case, this might be a serious emergency.

Something, indeed, must have been very, very wrong.

CHAPTER 9

Not many people knew it, seeing as how she mostly worked radar on the bridge, but Chakra was actually quite a skilled pilot. She had logged several thousand hours of training with the Air Force's best pilots after the war, and was ranked among the top pilots in the world. At least, she would have been if her very existence was not just as classified as the rest of Operation Red Dragon and the Kaiju.

She had been waiting for an opportunity to apply her piloting skills in service to the greater good for years, and the sudden appearance of the water Kaiju while her overprotective husband was away seemed as good an excuse as any. So, after tricking the hangar crew into believing she was acting on orders, she had stolen the experimental fighter which had been collecting dust in the *Akira*'s hangar for about a year, and flown out to try intercepting the encroaching sea monsters.

The new ship had been named *Kuroga*, or Black Moth, by its designer, Professor Toshiro, because the angular wings and forward-facing cockpit – a sphere which used gyroscopes to remain stable while the rest of the ship banked and spun – were vaguely similar in shape to a moth, and the fuselage was made of completely black material. It was a theory the Professor had that this unconventional combination of color and shape would make the ship invisible to radar, though it had yet to be properly tested, as this unique feature meant very little to creatures who did not use technology. Well, it might have worked against that giant bat in Romania, but he had yet to really bother anyone. Still, if this stealth technology worked, it would keep her from being detected by any airports in the city. If any ships in the water saw her, it would be written off as just another UFO sighting.

Chakra had pushed the fighter as fast as it could go to catch up with the creatures, and once they were in her sights, she fired the *Kuroga*'s twin Gatling guns at the churning water. After a few minutes of nonstop firing, she paused to judge the results.

For the life of her, she could not tell if she had any impact simply by looking at the water. The darn things were just below the surface, making it impossible to count how many there were with the naked eye. The noticeable swirl of red in the water behind them told her that she must have at least hit some of them, so perhaps she had thinned the herd a little, but she saw no sign of any dead bodies, and the swarm showed no sign of slowing down.

Chakra put the *Kuroga* in hover mode, which was accomplished by another experimental technique of putting the rotors on gyroscopic mounts embedded in the middle of the moth-like wings rather than on the front. She switched on the radar, and saw that some of the blue targets, perhaps fifteen or twenty, had indeed stopped moving.

She grinned, victoriously pumping her fist. That was better than she had expected. If she kept it up-

Suddenly, a pair of massive crocodilian jaws burst from the waves and snapped at the ship. Chakra swerved, avoiding disaster by inches, then fired at the offending beast. The barrage of bullets shredded the creature's throat, finishing it off.

After a quick mental scolding for making what she considered a rookie mistake, Chakra switched out of hover mode and continued her pursuit.

When she looked ahead, she could clearly see the skyline of Fukuoka fast approaching.

Now she was at a crossroads. The Red Dragons were under direct orders to remain hidden from the public, but they were also charged with keeping Kaiju away from populated areas. At this rate, it was looking like she would not be able to realize both goals simultaneously. She could not kill all of the Kaiju by herself before they reached Fukuoka, for she was just one pilot on her own. At the same time, she could not just abandon the chase and leave the city to its fate. Unlike her, the citizens of Fukuoka would not come back if they died.

No matter what choice she made, she dreaded the scolding that would come later from X, especially if she made any mistakes.

A glint of light came from the skyline. She squinted to see what it was.

Even with her sharp eyes, it was still hard to see any detail at such a distance, but she instantly recognized the object from its movement. That was the shuttle which carried Nancy and the reporter ahead of her, flying in full view of everyone in the city directly towards the coast. That meant they must have gotten her warning about the sea monsters and were doubling back to intercept them.

If the shuttle was not trying to hide, which appeared to be the case, that meant secrecy was no longer a priority, at least for the moment.

That settled the matter in her mind.

She stayed on course and continued firing into the water.

X could see the people below staring in awe as he and the shuttle shot through the skyline towards the coast. Under normal circumstances, being in view of the public would be considered a violation of protocol, but that hardly mattered to him now. This was not a normal circumstance; it was an ambush. Trying to stay hidden would just waste time. The people of Fukuoka had to be protected at any cost, even the cost of secrecy.

Ahead, he saw a black object hovering above the churning water, and recognized it as the *Kuroga* firing at the approaching Kaiju. Although it raised a lot of questions in his mind, since he had not ordered the fighter's launch, he decided that answers could wait. Whoever was in there was an ally, and that was what mattered until the threat was resolved.

A horde of arrow-like reptilian heads atop serpentine necks broke the water's surface like deadly harpoons reaching up for the onyx craft. One of them managed to clamp its jaws on the wing, but was not quite strong enough to overcome the upward pull of the rockets. The ship executed a barrel roll that lifted the serpent from the water and sent it hurtling through the air like a discarded tube sock.

Impressed, X made a mental note of the maneuver. Whoever was piloting the *Kuroga* was really good.

In the bay, beasts resembling especially large gharials pulled themselves ashore, guttural cries oozing from their unusually narrow jaws.

X flicked his wrists and caught his custom gun-swords in his hands.

He aimed and fired.

Richard watched in frightened awe from the shuttle as the Kaiju made landfall, but his concentration on the scene was broken by the hurried footsteps of General Tsujimori behind him. He turned, and watched as the old war vet stepped with clear determination out of the open hatch.

"What in the...?" Richard turned to Nancy, agog. "Does he have a parachute?!"

Nancy shook her head in the negative. "He doesn't need one."

Static filled the air again.

Lightning arced from General Tsujimori's entire body, reaching up to the shuttle and out to the metal within the buildings around him. The jagged blue-white bolts twisted and crisscrossed, forming the vague shape of a net which slowed his descent. It required less energy than he had expended to pull himself up to the shuttle earlier. He was not defying gravity here, but rather resisting it just enough to avoid injury when he landed.

Tsujimori never knew if electromagnetism was meant to be part of his power set or an unexpected side effect, but at times like this, he was glad it was there. Secretly, he also liked the dramatic flair it gave him as he descended from the heavens like an avenging angel on wings of lightning, and this time, he had an audience to witness it.

He came down at an angle, his goal to land as close to the bay as possible. If he could deliver a powerful enough strike to the water and fry the brutes in the bay, the problem would be nearly solved. Even if he did not kill the beasts, he would likely hurt them enough to send them running.

That was the ironic trait which predators and bullies had in common. They could inflict pain on others for eternity, but rarely could they take it themselves.

X was already blasting away at the creatures that had made it onto the land, so Tsujimori altered his trajectory away from their fight. Meanwhile, the pilot of the *Kuroga*, whoever it was, kept the monsters still in the water occupied. Excellent. The General would be met with little resistance on that front.

Once he was close enough to the street, he cut the power surging through his body and allowed himself to drop the remainder of the short distance. Once more on solid ground, he marched toward the shore. Walking was an unfortunate necessity for the moment, as he had to build his energy back up before he could deliver his finishing move. He paid no heed to the few citizens who had yet to flee, and were now staring in awe at both him and the spectacle playing out in the bay.

Still one block from the shore, he stopped dead in his tracks as he felt the ground begin to tremble.

He knew this kind of quake. It was coming from right below the street, like it had been in the clearing outside of the city mere moments ago.

Tsujimori's eyes widened in terror. "Oh, no…"

The street behind him burst open, and a veritable horde of dinosaurs erupted from the bowels of the Earth like lava.

The question of how and when the brutes had managed to dig tunnels beneath the city, though important, was not what immediately mattered. It was the nature of the attack itself that filled General Tsujimori with dread.

This was a coordinated attack from land and sea.

They were surrounded.

*****

Chakra whipped the *Kuroga* around as another set of jaws nearly closed on the wing. Though she had continued firing nonstop, the hail of bullets she rained down on them was not stopping the attack, or even slowing it down. They just kept coming, undeterred by the onslaught. On top of that, her ammunition was running low, so she would be defenseless soon.

Another Kaiju lunged straight for the cockpit, only to stop suddenly in midair as if it had gotten caught on something. Then it was pulled backwards faster than it had come, vanishing beneath the waves with a terrified expression on its face.

Chakra paused for a moment, confused by what had just happened.

She looked down through the *Kuroga*'s bubble cockpit at the water. One by one, she saw the Kaiju get yanked beneath the surface. In their place, a spreading plume of dark red tainted the sea until it filled her entire field of vision.

There was a mighty surge as something moved beneath the waves towards the city.

Something much larger than the beasts that had been attacking her.

The water parted for just an instant, revealing a pair of knifelike blades and rows of spines slicing through the surface.

A wide smile spread across her face, and her tail wagged excitedly, smacking against the back of her seat.

"It's him," she whispered in awe. "He's here!"

Pandemonium reigned in the streets.

The shuttle had risen up to a height where the Kaiju could not reach them, but it was still close enough for Richard to see everything. X and the General were surrounded, fighting for their lives as prehistoric nightmares poured from the ruined street. He could not even begin to count how many dinosaurs had emerged from the newly-formed crater, nor could he begin to identify all the different species on display.

Yet something about this turn of events scratched at his brain, for it made no sense to him. If the Kaiju were so bent on destroying cities, as Nancy had told him, why had they bypassed most of Fukuoka, getting to this point so close to the bay without causing any destruction along the way?

Unless...

The thought was one that he nearly dismissed as too absurd to believe, even for him, but that was only because he regarded reptiles as dumb, brutish creatures incapable of complex thought. That was bias, and he had conditioned himself to never succumb to personal bias. In the presence of his idol, it would be especially ill advised.

He hazarded to voice his thought out loud. "They planned this, didn't they?" he asked, still shocked by the very notion. "The dinosaurs planned an attack just so they could get X and the General. Right?"

"Impressive deduction," Armitage nodded, which prompted a shout of victory in Richard's mind. "And unfortunately true, from the looks of it. Unfortunately, the plan seems to be working. Even they might be overwhelmed by this many Kaiju at once."

Richard bit his lip as it struck him just how high the stakes were. "God help them, then."

As if on cue, a very low, yet eerily loud moan washed over the city. The entire world seemed to stop at the sound as everything and everyone froze in place. Even the raging battle below screeched to a halt, its participants turning towards the bay, where the sound had emanated from.

"Guys," said Nancy, who was staring out of the opposite window towards the sea. Her voice had a tinge of anticipation in it. "You'll want to see this."

The water boiled with intense heat, then swelled as if rising to form a mountain. A thick mask of steam filled the air.

A large Plesiosaur attempted to drag itself out of the water in a blind panic, its diamond-shaped flippers scraping uselessly against the smooth concrete of the pier.

The cloud of steam parted, and the mountain of water fell, creating waves that crashed upon the shoreline with tremendous fury.

And there he stood, burning bright red like a living pillar of magma.

He opened his mouth and roared. It was a terrible, primal sound. A cry from the very dawn of time itself. The call of a god made flesh.

At his cry, the air trembled, and windows all across the city of Fukuoka shattered into fine powder.

All who heard this horrible sound, whether human or Kaiju, knew in an instant just how tiny and pathetic they really were.

"Th-That..." Richard stammered as he beheld the arisen titan. "Not a dinosaur... It... It..."

"*He,* Richard," Nancy corrected, even though she was every bit as amazed as him. She reached up to grab the cross which dangled from her necklace. "That one's a 'he'.

"And his name is Kozerah."

CHAPTER 10

Nothing else in the whole world equaled the majesty of Kozerah. At least, that was what Richard thought as he watched the beast wade through the bay towards Fukuoka. He drank in every detail as the giant approached.

It – no, he; Nancy had said the beast was a "he" – was clearly reptilian, but he was most definitely not a dinosaur. His shimmering scaly skin was smooth and so red that he almost looked as though he were made of fire. His snout was long and pointed, more akin to a lizard or a snake than the dinosaurs below. A pair of long viper-like fangs hung from his upper jaw, and when coupled with the twin knifelike horns above his eyes, he almost looked demonic. Yellow armor plating covered the front of his torso, and as the shuttle orbited around him to a new angle, the short serrated spikes on his back came into view. These gradually gave way to a single row of needle-like quills that ran down the length of his long, sinewy tail, at the end of which was an array of curved spikes arranged like the petals of a deadly flower. His arms and legs were thin compared to the rest of him but looked surprisingly muscular in spite of this. Both of his large hands sported three long fingers and an opposable thumb, each capped with a sharp fishhook claw as black as night. The three-toed feet that rose from the bay were like Egyptian pyramids stamping themselves into the ground.

There were two details in particular that really impacted Richard. First was how incredibly massive Kozerah was. True, the other Kaiju he had seen were large, but Kozerah towered above them all. Judging by the buildings, he was at least two-hundred-and-fifty feet tall, maybe taller. It was difficult to wrap his head around, even as he was seeing it with his own eyes.

The second detail was how eerily human Kozerah looked in spite of his reptilian nature. His posture was completely upright, not hunched over like the dinosaurs, with his arms hanging at his sides, and the eyes....

The eyes...

Richard had seen plenty of lizards, snakes, and crocodiles over the course of his life, and he knew them to be dull creatures. To look into the black slits most lizards had for pupils revealed that very little was happening behind them. A lizard had no higher thoughts beyond seeking whatever it needed to survive.

But looking into Kozerah's eyes, which were every bit as reptilian as the rest of him, Richard saw intelligence as plain as day, but it was not human intelligence. No, what he saw was a different kind of intelligence, the kind he could not even begin to comprehend, and likely never would.

It was this detail which filled Richard's heart with fear for the whole human race.

From the corner of his eye, he saw X and General Tsujimori leave the battle, retreating deeper into the city.

"Where the heck are they going?" he asked, a bit shocked at the retreat. "What about that red thing? Aren't they going to fight it?"

Nancy laughed as if she found the statement adorably naïve. "There's no way either of them would stand a chance against Kozerah," she said. "Even if they could, they'd never fight him anyway. Their job is just to run crowd control now."

"What? Why not?"

"Because Kozerah's not our enemy, Richard." She pointed to the dinosaurs below. "He's theirs."

Kozerah bellowed a challenge at the horde before him. Just as all the demons in Hell knew God and trembled, so too did these creatures know and fear this mighty titan. If they were smart, they would leave the human settlement and not challenge him to a fight. Their brethren had tried that many times, even as recently as a few years ago, when Kozerah had descended from the sacred mountain, and it had not ended well for them.

Yet none of the Kaiju in the city fled. Instead, the horde responded by roaring back in unison, declaring their intention to fight. It seemed they thought their strength was in their numbers.

Kozerah grunted half in resignation, half in disappointment. Some creatures just never learned.

The ceratopsians in the horde charged, horns aimed low at Kozerah's ankles, the intent to cripple him all too clear.

With the grace, but not the form, of a martial arts master, Kozerah spun on his feet. His mighty tail swung out, tearing up the pavement as it went, and caught the charging line in one blow, sweeping them into a nearby hotel as a broom may sweep away dust.

As he turned back again, he was caught off guard when the sauropods, who came the closest to equaling his tremendous stature, reared up and wrapped their long necks around his limbs and torso, binding him.

Kozerah was surprised at how effective the sauropods' attack was. He struggled against them but could not move or break their hold. They had caught him in just the right way to make movement difficult.

Following close behind them, the tyrannosaurs leapt like panthers, clamping their jaws on him wherever they happened to land, their teeth sinking into his thick flesh, though no bite was quite deep enough to draw blood.

Kozerah closed his eyes and clenched his fists.

His red skin began to pulse with light, slowly at first, but growing quicker with each second.

The air around him rippled with intense heat.

One by one, the dinosaurs released their grips on him, smoke rising from their seared flesh as they pulled away.

Kozerah's mouth twisted into something which, on a human face, might have been a triumphant smile. These creatures could only be a challenge to him for so long.

The wounded beasts began to retreat, only to be stopped when a web of lightning arced between the buildings, stopping them dead in their tracks. They turned for a different route through the city, only to recoil as a flying human draped in black peppered them with bullets. The combined attack kept the horde in Kozerah's sights, forcing them into a close huddle.

It seemed to Kozerah that the humans had corralled the brutes into one place so he could finish them off in one blow.

Very well.

He felt the energy course through his veins as he channeled it where it needed to go. His horns flickered with light that grew steadily brighter and brighter.

He inhaled deeply.

When he exhaled, his breath was a brilliant stream of violet flame.

The ray washed over the mass of prehistoric nightmares and culminated in a blinding explosion that rocked the city for miles around.

Then it was over. The beam vanished, and nothing remained where it had struck but charred bones and a wide patch of ground that smoldered with ash and melted tar.

Kozerah turned his gaze heavenward and bellowed a victorious roar that shook the shuttle above him. This completed, he turned and wandered back into the sea. There was little reason to stay now that the threat was gone.

Fighting the dinosaurs was child's play. Kozerah almost felt like battling them by himself was unfair.

Almost.

Besides, the only way to stop their constant attacks was to destroy their masters, and he knew the day that they would finally take to the battlefield themselves was close.

Beyond the horizon, he could sense one of them already stirring, heading for a different continent on the other side of the ocean. He was too far away to deal with that one.

His allies there would just have to take care of it.

CHAPTER 11

As he flew high above the island, CIGOR's blue eye detected nothing but wreckage in the water around Rabu Nii. No human signatures registered below; not that he was surprised. The Kaiju of this island were incredibly dangerous, hence the quarantine. The humans who had landed here were long dead already.

Strangely, there was more debris than a small research vessel should have left behind, and the pieces looked incongruous with each other, as if they came from different vessels. He switched his scan to a higher resolution, and saw a broken panel knocking against an offshore rock. It bore the unmistakable emblem of the United States Navy he had seen so often at sea. A distress signal must have been sent from the *Delta*, and the Navy ship, whatever kind it had been – the debris was so mangled that even CIGOR's enhanced vision could not identify it – had sailed to its doom with the best of intentions.

CIGOR had half a mind to descend upon the island and unleash vengeance upon the murderous beasts that resided there. Though the prehistoric Kaiju were all hostile toward mankind, the creatures on Rabu Nii had been left alone because the place was so isolated. Rabu Nii had been stricken from all official maps, and the waters around it were considered a Q-zone. Since the dinosaurs never went into the water, and would have been unable to swim very far even if they did, they were essentially trapped.

However, Kaiju that attacked humans were to be punished without mercy. As both a member of Operation Red Dragon and as one of humanity's caretakers, CIGOR was not about to let this heinous act stand without delivering swift retribution.

Yet when he scanned the island, it was devoid of any Kaiju signatures.

This absence was very disturbing. The place should have been teeming with those wretched monsters, and yet there were none.

CIGOR checked his memory against the databanks and geographical information again. He was definitely on the right island.

So where were the Kaiju?

He scanned again, this time for anomalies, and that was when he found the sinkholes.

Rabu Nii was pockmarked with large, perfectly round openings leading deep underground which had not been there when the island had been checked last month.

In addition, the volcano at the island's center showed all the signs of eruption except for lava. Of course, CIGOR knew that an eruption here was impossible, as Rabu Nii's volcano had been extinct for ages. Yet something had clearly come out of it, and it had come out recently.

He noticed indentations in the crumbled rocks on the mountainside. They were evenly spaced apart, rounded at the back with three prongs at the front.

He knew what these were.

Footprints.

Footprints larger than any normal Kaiju would leave.

Suddenly, the pieces all came together in CIGOR's mind. Legends and myths had said that the master of the dinosaurs, a beast named Allorex, resided somewhere in this island chain, but no evidence had been found to suggest Rabu Nii was the place.

However, a thorough search had never been carried out. The resident Kaiju had been too ravenous to allow it. So the island had simply been quarantined.

The creatures on this island had not been trapped. They had been protecting their slumbering master.

And now their master was awake.

All this time Operation Red Dragon had left Rabu Nii alone, and they should have been taking measures to wipe it off the map literally as well as metaphorically.

The sinkholes were tunnels. The dinosaurs were travelling underground, and CIGOR had no clue where they were heading yet.

He flew back to the *Akira* as fast as his rocket could push him.

Michael Sun awoke and instantly felt that something was amiss, but he could not figure out what it was.

He flicked on the light beside his bed, rubbed his eyes, and looked around his bedroom. Nothing looked out of place. He got up, stretched, and walked to the window, slowly drawing the curtains to look outside.

Beyond his window stretched the deserts of Nevada, looking the same as they had since he had arrived three months prior. Nothing wrong there, either.

He glanced at his reflection in the mirror that hung on the closet door. Aside from looking like he had just awoken, which was to be expected, he still saw no evidence of anything wrong.

He grabbed the glass of water on the nightstand, and was just about ready to write off his unnamable unease as the product of some nightmare he could not recall when he turned on the TV across from his bed. What greeted him was a news report of a disaster which had struck

Fukuoka, Japan, complete with grainy but unmistakable footage of two men he knew quite well fighting dinosaurs in the streets.

Fury boiled through Michael's veins at the sight. He gripped the glass in his hand so tightly that it started to crack.

Though he was alone, his rage needed an outlet, so he began to yell, "Those sons of-" before a new image stopped the final offending word in his throat.

The image was a red dragon – a *real* red dragon – marching into the city.

Kozerah.

Michael Sun had never seen Kozerah before, but he had heard stories, spoken to eyewitnesses. Amongst all the monsters roaming the planet, Kozerah was unique. This could only be him.

The glass fell from his hand, landing on the bed and spilling its contents on the sheets.

Chakra had missed her opportunity to sneak out of the hangar before everyone else returned to the *Akira*. In fact, she had landed the *Kuroga* at the exact same time as the shuttle.

She had hoped that the events of the day would have sent everyone springing into action elsewhere on the ship, allowing her to skulk away without being seen and get back to her station with no one the wiser. Unfortunately for her, X and General Tsujimori wanted to commend the mystery pilot for his-or-her bravery in taking the experimental craft into battle, or maybe deliver a verbal thrashing for insubordination.

Just her luck either way.

She had opened the rear hatch but had yet to descend. She knew that X would probably be angry. She did not fear repercussions from him – he would never maliciously hurt her – but disappointment in betraying trust could be the most damaging thing in a relationship like theirs. Depending on how he took this…

She shook her head, banishing the thought. No secret could be kept forever. If she did not reveal herself now, someone on the bridge would eventually tell them when she had run off, and X would easily fill in the blanks from there. It would be better to come clean on her own here and now.

Maybe.

She descended from the *Kuroga* slowly, like a condemned prisoner being led to the gallows, eyes focused on the floor, ears drooping, tail tucked sheepishly between her legs.

Chakra spared a quick glance up. She did not see the General's expression. She was focused entirely on X, trying to figure out what he was thinking.

Unfortunately, his face was completely unreadable. He might have been shocked, enraged, or having a heart attack. For all she knew, he was comatose. Her eyes shot back to the floor.

"Sorry," she said sheepishly, tears welling up in her eyes as the shame of her actions increased. "I know you don't-"

Her vision was suddenly obscured by black cloth, and she felt arms wrap gently around her.

X drew her close to him in a hug, saying nothing.

She allowed herself to relax and melt into his warm, comforting embrace.

*****

"You called that thing Kozerah," Richard said as he followed Nancy and Dr. Armitage out of the hangar. His adrenaline was still pumping, and his mind was racing with questions. "Why did you call him that?"

Armitage made a small sweeping gesture with his hand as he shrugged. "Because that is his name, Mr. Godfrey," he said, as if the answer were obvious.

Richard shook his head. "Alright, let me put it this way: *Why* did you name him that?"

"We didn't," Nancy replied.

Richard blinked, confused. "What? You said his name was Kozerah!"

"Yes, we did."

"So why did you call him that?"

"Like the good doctor said, that's his name."

Richard sighed loudly. This was getting *very* frustrating. "Look, this Kozerah is the first monster I've heard anyone refer to by a proper name, not just as a species. There's got to be a reason for that, so what is it?"

Nancy shrugged. "We call him that because that's his name, Richard."

"That's not an answer! That's hyperbole! Where did the name come from? For heaven's sake, give me a straight answer for once!"

Nancy stopped and turned on a dime to stare right into Richard's eyes, her calm demeanor having given way to offense. "*Excuse me?*" She jabbed her finger into his chest. "I've given you plenty of straight answers since we shanghaied you!"

Armitage blinked, though his face remained stoic and his tone changed only slightly to express his surprise. "You *shanghaied* him?"

Nancy, remembering that Armitage did not know how they had gotten to Richard, adjusted her collar nervously. "We believe in efficiency," she said, hoping that answer was enough.

"I'll admit," Richard said, "that you have explained a lot to me, but it feels like for every question that gets a clear answer, another two show up that get nothing but double talk or rain checks! I feel like Hercules fighting the Hydra! I'm clearly on this ship because you want me to see all this absurdity, so why not just tell me everything that's going on and be done with it?"

Nancy stepped closer to him, her eyes narrowing. "I tell you *what* you need to know, *when* you need to know it, and I *always* let a sufficient amount of time pass for you to process what you've learned."

"Process?"

"I know everyone you've met so far acts real casual about the 'absurdity', as you call it, but that's because we live this stuff every day. You, on the other hand, had never seen anything even remotely paranormal for yourself before we picked you up and brought you aboard. You just trusted that it was real, and that the answers would somehow make sense to you when you got them. Well, Richard, the only way those answers will ever make sense is if you have time to accept them first."

She pointed in the general direction of the city. "The people in Fukuoka just got a very rough introduction to the true nature of the world. We've eased *you* into it as gently as possible."

Armitage cocked an eyebrow. "By kidnapping him?"

"I'm trying to win an argument here, Daisuke!"

"He's made it this far, and he's seen Kozerah with his own eyes." Armitage nodded approvingly at Richard. "I'd say he is adjusting well enough. Perhaps we should be a bit more forthwith about Kozerah."

Silence fell over the trio.

"The easiest way to put it," Nancy eventually said, "is to say that Kozerah is essentially a god."

"A god?" Richard blinked in astonished confusion. He had enough knowledge of folklore and mythology to know what a god was, but Kozerah did not fit his mental image. "You mean like Zeus or Thor?"

"Try Cthulhu," Nancy replied. "I guess we're due for another trip to the archives. Come on."

As the trio headed for the archives once again, Richard kept pace with Armitage. "Thanks for that," he said.

Armitage nodded. "Of course. I am pleased to know your mind is as strong as ever. You truly are just the man for this job."

"What job?"

Armitage lowered his head slightly, though his expression remained unaltered. Richard was starting to wonder if the man had any emotions at all. "Though I took your side just now, Miss Boardwalk is nonetheless correct," he said. "Sometimes the truth is best served in small doses over time. It is important that you not know your full role just yet. As a reporter, I am sure you know that you must get the whole story before you set it down on paper. Moving forward, you must apply that mindset to this little adventure."

Coming from his mentor, Richard took this lack of an answer somewhat better than he might have taken it from Nancy.

CHAPTER 12

Across the ocean, on the coast of Chile, a small fishing village sat in the foothills of the Andes mountain range. It was called Boca de Vacca, and there was really nothing special about it at all. Only one thing of significance ever happened there, and it occurred in 1964, mere hours after Kozerah had defeated the Kaiju in Fukuoka.

The sun was just starting to sink beneath the horizon, and the town was still buzzing with activity as though it were midday. None of the people there were prepared for the deadly swarm of black hornets that flew in from the sea.

There were hundreds of these hornets, each angular exoskeleton bigger than a car, and their stingers were aimed like guns at the village. Worst of all, they were not alone.

Behind them, marching through the offshore waters as if it were a wading pool, was a beast unlike anything the villagers had ever seen before. It should have been another insect, like a beetle or a ladybug, but its upright posture made its two-hundred-foot frame look vaguely humanoid as it swaggered towards shore. The exoskeleton was a sickly olive green and segmented in odd patterns that made it look like a suit of armor. The arms seemed longer than they ought to have been, brushing the water as they swayed back and forth, and below the elbows, they appeared to be metallic, glinting a dull shade of silver in the fading sunlight. The shell on its back hung like a cape worn by an emperor.

The head was especially curious. The multifaceted eyes were yellow orbs which wrapped around the sides of the cranium, lacking pupils or eyelids, yet somehow the human onlookers in the village could tell that the beast was staring at them. Above these eyes were a pair of horns that might have been mandibles if the beast crawled on its belly like a normal bug, but since it stood upright, they looked more like the horns of the Devil. Lastly was a jagged x-shaped pattern that opened like a mouth, from which emanated a deep staccato roar. It raised one of its metallic hands, which ended in a shallow bowl tipped with three short, sharp prongs, and roared again. It looked almost like a general ordering his soldiers to charge.

Upon hearing this terrible sound, the people of Boca de Vacca turned to run, instinctively heading to the Andes as they might when faced with a deadly oncoming storm. To some in the crowd, it seemed a pointless retreat since the hornets were approaching so fast that there was no chance of outrunning them. It seemed even more hopeless when balls of red fire shot from their stingers, bursting on the street and the buildings, raining debris upon the terrified villagers.

Ear-piercing screeches swept down from the mountains, stopping the crowd's retreat even as another red orb burst in front of them.

The source was easy enough to see. Descending from the peaks of the Andes, moving in a terrifying synchronized murmuration, were more enormous bird-like creatures than anyone in the crowd could count.

As they drew closer, the crowd could tell that the creatures were not really birds at all, but looked more like Pterosaurs. Their mighty wings and lithe bodies were covered by a leathery hide rather than feathers. Their long, sharp beaks came in all shapes and sizes, some sporting horns, others lined with rows of sharp teeth.

One man in the crowd, who had once been a pilot before his helicopter had been destroyed in 1952, trembled at the sight and made the Sign of the Cross over his chest.

"Dios mio," Carlos Hernandez whispered in abject horror. "Not again…"

The mumuration twisted and dove. For an instant, it seemed as if they, too, might attack the defenseless crowd.

At the last moment, the pterosaurs collectively swooped upward, the rush of wind stripping the shingles from rooftops and knocking many an onlooker to the ground. With incredible force, the pterosaurs plowed into the hornets, and the sky erupted in a furious battle of talons ripping through exoskeletons and stingers piercing through wings.

The villagers were not so awestruck by the sight that they had any desire to see the battle play out, at least not while they were still right below it. With the hornets distracted, the humans could continue running to safety, and they did, even more panicked than they were before. Since the mountains were no longer safe, they scattered in random directions, running anywhere that seemed like it might offer them some kind of shelter from the apocalyptic battle in the sky.

Carlos dared to glance upwards when a heavy shadow fell over the town.

Above was another pterosaur, only this one was bigger.

So much bigger.

He remembered this one as well.

The master of the bugs assessed the situation from the safety of the water.

He had led this assault himself to prove his worth to the other masters. The insects were considered inferior to the dinosaurs and sea monsters. If he were the first to lead a successful attack against the humans, he knew his kind would be treated differently. Perhaps they would have the advantage when the world was restored to the way it had been.

Things had turned bad quickly, though. His hornets had been caught off guard by the pterosaurs, and now their master, the traitor, was coming to confront him directly, and she had the unfair advantage of flight. Though he had managed to spit a few fireballs at her, she had dodged them effortlessly, and countered with fire of her own that scorched his shell.

He turned and fled quickly back into the sea, ducking beneath the waves before the traitor could lay a claw on him.

This was not cowardice, he thought. This was strategy. This was practical. He could fight any of the other masters under the right circumstances.

These simply were not the right circumstances.

Retreat was the only option. His hornets would simply have to fend for themselves. They were drones, anyway. No great loss.

It was more important that *he* survive to achieve victory later.

"We need to talk about earlier."

X sounded serious, but his tone showed no anger as yet. He and Chakra had gone straight to their quarters from the hangar, neither one speaking or releasing the other until the door was closed. This was a new behavior for X, who was resistant to public displays of affection, especially while on duty. That he had held her in his arms with little regard for his own image was a new development that Chakra liked.

Any romantic mood that might have sprung from it, however, dissolved as soon as they were alone, which was the inverse of what usually happened.

"I don't want you pulling a stunt like that again," X continued. "You're sitting out the next fight, and whatever fights happen after it."

Chakra sighed in exasperation. "Why?" she asked. "Didn't I handle myself well enough out there? *I* sure thought so, especially since the *Kuroga*'s never been tested in combat before."

"I agree. You performed excellently out there and proved the *Kuroga*'s worth in battle. Even so, you're not doing it again."

"And again I ask, why?"

"Because you'll be safe here on the *Akira*."

Chakra could not suppress a laugh. "Safe? From what, dying? X, I'm like you, remember? I can't die! You do know how many times I've been killed since we first met, right?"

"Yes, and I've hated every time it's happened!"

X's reply stopped the argument for a moment. There had been a raw emotion in his voice when he spoke those words that belied his gruff exterior. To Chakra's canine ears, he sounded vulnerable, which was an emotion even she had never heard from him before.

His head hung low. "I know you'll come back to life no matter what," he said as softly as his rough voice would allow, "but every time you die..." He sat on their bed, averting his eyes from his wife. "Chakra, I *hate* seeing you die. Even though I know you'll come back, I hate it. I hate even *thinking* about it." He looked up, his glowing eyes staring deep into hers. "I'm a soldier. Seeing people I care about die in battle is part of my job, and I have no illusions about that. But you're my *wife*, Chakra. I never want you to be in that kind of danger." His eyes lowered again. "It cuts me deeper than anything else in this world."

Chakra plopped herself down next to X and snuggled up close to him. "It's not much fun for me, either. I'm pretty sure I saw Saint Peter roll his eyes at me last time I kicked it." It was a half-hearted joke, but it did seem to soften X ever so slightly, so she continued. "I worry about you too, you know, but I've never stopped you from doing what you have to do. You've devoted your life to saving the world, and you use your powers to do it. All I want is a chance to do the same thing. I don't want to think that I endured all those years of torture on the island just so I could sit on the sidelines."

She placed her hand under his bearded chin and tilted his head up so she could look him in the eye once more. "Besides, Kozerah showed up today. He hasn't shown up anywhere in years. That tells me the situation is getting pretty dire. You'll need all the help you can get, right? Well, I can help." She smiled sweetly. "We're the same, X. We were both made for this, as much as we were made for each other. So let me help you next time, okay? Please?"

X's mouth curled in such a way that was almost a smile. "I'll have to sleep on it," he said.

Chakra's tail wagged as she grinned and drew closer to him, picking up on his hint.

Meanwhile, in the small theater, Richard was about to receive his answers about Kozerah, and he had no idea how profoundly they would change his outlook on the entire world. He was once again seated beside Nancy, while Daisuke Armitage stood apart from them and leaned against the wall.

"You'll have to excuse the poor quality," Nancy said as the reel began to play. "This was filmed in the early days, after all. Nineteen Fifty-two, to be exact."

The image was, to Richard's surprise, in full color, though the shakiness of the footage did make the image occasionally hard to see. In the moments when it steadied, he saw Kozerah descending the slopes of Mount Fuji, grappling with a group of four dinosaurs. The shot was filmed from above, likely from one of the shuttles, if he had to guess.

"We first learned about the big ones in Forty-nine, but we didn't find them until Fifty-two, when groups of the smaller Kaiju started assembling in certain areas all over the world. Best as we can tell, they were staging some sort of coup by catching Kozerah and the others off guard."

Richard's head whipped from the screen to Nancy so quickly that he nearly gave himself whiplash. "Others?!? There are more Kozerahs out there?"

"Sort of."

The reel switched, and before him was another aerial shot, somewhere in a rocky desert mountain range. Whatever titan was in this video nearly blended in with the sand and rocks around him, but Richard could see that it was covered in spikes and beating the tar out of some truly massive scorpions.

Nancy continued to exposit. "Like I told you earlier, 'Kaiju' is just a general term, Japanese for 'strange beast'. They can be any size, really. The big ones are their masters. Some of us call them Daikaiju, giant strange beasts. You've seen Kozerah." She pointed to the spiky behemoth on the screen. "That's Armadagger."

The reel switched again, showing a flock of pterosaurs flying towards a snowcapped mountain range, led by one of their own who was much bigger than the rest.

"And that's Andrea," Nancy continued, "and her charges, the Pterosaurs."

Richard scratched his head. He was amazed by the sight of these giants, but something was bothering him that he could not quite piece together. He struggled to put it into words. "So, these big ones are on our side?" No, that wasn't quite what was bothering him, but it was a good question either way.

"It would be more accurate," said Daisuke Armitage, "to say that we are on their side."

"You mean because they're gods?"

Armitage, who was leaning on the doorframe, shook his head. "They're not literally gods, no. God*like*, to be certain. They are dragons, who are in a league all their own. They were here at the beginning of time, and shall be here at the end of it."

In any other circumstance, Richard might have taken the doctor's words as pertaining to myth, but he could not fully dismiss the notion that they were meant to be literal. After all he had been through, Richard had no trouble believing it. "But aren't dragons evil?" he asked. "In all the classic myths I've ever read, I've never come across a friendly depiction of a dragon."

"They were not considered evil in Asia," Armitage replied. "In China and Japan, dragons were the wise protectors of humanity. In a way, we are their charges.

"I wish I could tell you more about their origins," he sighed. "Sadly, we can no better espouse on that topic than we can on the origins of life itself. Accounts of the Daikaiju go back to the earliest days of recorded history, and they likely predate even that. The ancient texts are where we learned their names. Even in those, it would seem the Daikaiju named themselves, rather than being named by us."

Richard nodded in understanding, but something still bothered him. "How many of these big ones are there?" Another good question, but still not quite the one he was trying to ask.

"Not as many as the small ones," Nancy answered, "but one Daikaiju has the power of at least a thousand Kaiju, and they don't all have our best interests at heart."

The reel presented new images, these ones static. They were lined up together, and from left to right, they showed a cave painting of an especially large theropod dinosaur, a fleeting glimpse of a vaguely insectoid thing with oddly-shaped hands that reminded Richard of sporks, a thing slipping through the water that might have been a fish or an iguana, and something that looked to Richard like an alligator with horns glued to its body.

"Again, sorry for the poor quality, but the big ones have been elusive up until recently." Nancy rose and pointed to the pictures in left-to-right order. "These four are the ones that currently have our attention, the masters of the dinos and bugs that you've seen. This cave painting depicts Allorex, the bug with sporks for hands is Exoskel, the fish-lizard is Barracudasaurus, and the resplendent alligator is Wanirah. Based on all of the evidence, these four are the masterminds behind the destruction we've seen so far." She gave a signal to the booth, and the projector switched off. "Based on our research, these four used to regard each other as enemies, but it seems the only thing they hate more than each other is us, so at the moment, they're united until humanity is out of the equation. So, you were kind of right earlier: some dragons are evil."

Richard nodded, but something was still bothering him. "So, wait, if that Pterosaur one-"

"Andrea."

"Yeah, her. If she's also prehistoric, how come she doesn't have it in for us too? Shouldn't she be with the dinosaurs?" No, still not quite what was bothering him.

"Pterosaurs aren't dinosaurs, Mr. Godfrey," Armitage replied.

"No, but neither are bugs or sea monsters."

Nancy shrugged. "Andrea defected. We don't know exactly why. Our best guess is that she figured the pterosaurs would stand a better chance at survival if she sided with humanity's protectors. I don't blame her, either. Kozerah is one heck of a juggernaut."

"Fair enough," Richard said. "I guess the important thing is that she's on our side, right?"

Nancy laughed. "You couldn't be more wrong, Richard. Like the good doctor just said, they're not on our side. We're on their side. It's not the place of Man to tell God what to do."

Richard nodded, scratched his head, and in a flash, he suddenly knew what had been bothering him. "Nineteen Fifty-two!" he exclaimed. "You said that's when Kozerah, Andrea, and Arm-and-hammer-"

"Armadagger."

"Right, him. You said that's when they first appeared, right?"

"Yes, starting on December 15."

"I remember the reports. Some eyewitnesses saying monsters had shown up, but they fell off the radar, and the official word wrote the destruction off as natural disasters. But it was really those three!" Richard turned to Daisuke Armitage. "They appeared a week after you...spoke at my...college..."

In his mind, Richard set up a corkboard on which were posted all of the strange things that had happened both to him and to the world at large. Mental strands of thread began stretching between each item, twisting and linking in ways that Richard had never thought of before. By the end, his mental corkboard looked like a deranged art project concocted by a paranoid conspiracy theorist, and yet the connections all made perfect sense.

He stood, still staring at Armitage in utter disbelief. "You... You knew what would happen, didn't you? That the Daikaiju were going to wake up, and that I'd be in the audience to hear you speak that day. Somehow, you knew."

Armitage was as stone faced as ever, but his voice had a knowing, almost coy tone to it as he replied. "Hmm. Quite an absurd notion, isn't it, Mr. Godfrey?"

CHAPTER 13

Michael Sun had spent the whole day fielding calls. Those representatives at the United Nations who knew about Operation Red Dragon were livid about the recent attacks in Japan and South America, especially considering how Operation Red Dragon had failed to contain them properly. He had caught all of their anger, and now *he* was angry, but with no outlet upon which to vent his anger.

His contact had been right. Those freaks were clearly planning to go public with the whole thing. Mike even suspected that they had deliberately botched things in Fukuoka and left Boca de Vacca to its fate for just that purpose. The news was already lit up with coverage, filled with speculation from people who claimed to be experts, many expressing skepticism about the veracity of the footage and eyewitness testimonies. Since none of them were involved with Operation Red Dragon, Mike knew these so-called experts were nothing but clueless fame-seekers, but he welcomed their skepticism as long as it helped keep a lid on things until he could find a way to fix this.

If the Red Dragons weren't going to keep things quiet, *somebody* had to.

Yet the appearances of Kozerah and Andrea after all these years implied something else to him, something he did not want to acknowledge as true so he could continue being mad at them. If those two had surfaced, the predictions made by their scientists had been correct: the world was indeed heading towards some sort of large-scale Kaiju event, which meant that things were about to get very bad very fast.

In that case, the machine would have to be launched, whether it was ready or not, for the sake of all mankind.

Mike sat on the unmarked private bus that ferried people back and forth between Groom Lake and civilization, silently urging it to move faster so he could get to the secret base sooner. His personal hatred for the place had taken a backseat to the urgency of recent global events.

He was just thinking about what sort of harsh, scathing things he would say the next time he called X and General Tsujimori when the bus plowed hard into something on the road, jolting him as violently from his thoughts as from his seat. The impact point was low and should have simply stopped the bus in its tracks, yet as he tumbled forward, Mike felt the vehicle's rear end rise toward the heavens and continue forward, as if whatever had struck the bus was flipping it.

Time seemed to slow as the bus hung inverted above the street, its occupants tumbling end over end.

Another flip so it was upright once more, and the bus slammed hard back onto the road, the last scraps of its momentum giving out as the wheels splayed outward and the underside scraped the pavement.

Mike was dazed, having been knocked against several benches, the ceiling, and at least two other people. He might have remained on the floor to recover, but the sudden appearance of a thick bony horn piercing the hull right before his face snapped him into fight-or-flight mode.

But there was nowhere to run. Similar horns stabbed both sides of the bus. Through the windows, he could see scaly arched backs that could only belong to the dinosaurs.

Mike joined the other passengers huddled in the center, and saw from the corner of his eye that the rear emergency exit of the bus had popped open, and was unguarded.

"Head for the back!" he shouted to the other passengers. "Get out and run like the devil himself is after you!"

The passengers heeded his command, and were fortunate to escape unmolested by the Kaiju, which Mike had a feeling were triceratopses, or some similar species.

Mike made sure everyone else got off before he did, but as he ran for the exit himself, the dinosaurs pressed their attack, making him stumble and twist his ankle as he ran.

Through the back, he saw the other passengers escaping, and not a single Kaiju was in pursuit.

That made no sense. These Kaiju hated humans and wanted them all dead. The bus was not their enemy, and they must have seen the others running. There was no way to miss them. This was the Nevada desert, a vast expanse of nothing for miles around, so any human caught here would be a sitting duck.

Mike finally staggered through the exit and began limping away as fast as he could go.

He paused when he realized that the sound of the bus being destroyed had stopped.

He turned and saw that the army of ceratopsians had abandoned the bus and were now focused on him, slowly encircling him like sharks. There was no way he could move fast enough to evade them, and the other passengers were already too far away to help him.

What on Earth were the monsters doing singling him out like this?

A thought struck him, and though it seemed too absurd to be true, the evidence before his eyes was undeniable.

The Kaiju had let the others go and continued attacking the bus when he was still in it.

Now that he was out, they had abandoned the bus and turned their attention towards him.

They were targeting him specifically.

Oh God…

Michael Sun slowly sank to his knees. He knew in that moment he was going to die right then and there, and knowing how vicious the dinosaurs could be, there would probably be nothing left of him to bury.

He took a deep breath in an attempt to steady his nerves.

If he was going to die today, he may as well face his fate with some dignity.

He closed his eyes and spread his arms to expose his chest, waiting for the beasts to gore him with their horns.

His eyes opened again when he felt the ground trembling from below.

The street before him heaved upward, peeling away to reveal a massive, mottled brown carapace covered in ivory spikes.

As it had on the bus, time seemed to slow as Mike drank in the details of the arisen titan. At a guess, it was perhaps a hundred and fifty feet tall, though its humanoid posture was slouched. The backs of his hands, tops of his feet, elbows, knees, the top of his head, and top of his short tail sported segments of spiky carapace similar to that on his back. The head was broad and flat, with a pointed snout and large eyes that glared down at him. The skin not covered by shell was smooth and sand-colored, making it hard to tell if he was reptilian or mammalian. Though the resemblance was superficial at best, the completed image reminded Mike of an armadillo.

He knew the beast's proper name, though.

Armadagger.

The ceratopsians charged the new challenger, their original task of murdering Mike abandoned.

With movements oddly similar to a raging gorilla, Armadagger pounded at the ground, slamming the armored backs of his hands down on his attackers.

For a moment, Mike noticed that Armadagger was slowly backing away, and the dinosaurs were following him, taking the chaos of the fight from where he knelt. It seemed a deliberate move, as if Armadagger was herding the beasts away to save him.

Was he imagining it? Was it just his terror playing tricks on his mind?

No, of course not. Though he had never seen one, he still knew from the files that Armadagger was a Daikaiju, and Daikaiju were more than just mindless beasts. It *had* to be deliberate.

The fight was over in a few minutes, and the Daikaiju was the proud victor. Armadagger roared triumphantly to the sky. It was a warbling sound that was heard clearly in towns several miles away.

With the enemy sufficiently pulverized, Armadagger began to dig, tossing sand and rock into the air like a dog burying a bone, and almost as suddenly as he had appeared, he was gone.

Michael Sun stayed rooted to the spot where he knelt on the ruined road, staring at the newly formed crater surrounded by dinosaur carcasses. It was like a scene straight out of a prehistoric horror movie. He did not know how much time passed between the end of the fight and the time the black helicopter from Groom Lake arrived, no doubt investigating the disturbance.

Armadagger had saved him from what was, for all intents and purposes, an assassination attempt.

Michael Sun now had a greater understanding of what was really going on.

CHAPTER 14

General Ishiro Tsujimori had secretly been monitoring all communications being sent and received by the *Akira* since his discussion with X in the hopes of catching the informant, and his patience had finally paid off. While going over the transmission records with the communications officers, he had determined a pattern of who was aboard the ship and where the individuals in question were whenever messages were sent from the private conference rooms.

Fortune had smiled upon him, for he had been alerted to another transmission in the wee small hours of the morning.

There was only one person who could be in the private conference room at that moment, and General Tsujimori already knew who it was by process of elimination. Nancy Boardwalk was with Armitage and Richard, which he had confirmed for himself, while Chakra and X were…otherwise occupied. Only one other person on the whole ship had access.

He had ordered the hallway to be clear of personnel until otherwise stated. If, heaven forbid, the situation turned violent, he did not want anyone caught in the crossfire. He also did not want to convey the perception that there was disharmony amongst the commanding officers on the ship, which would be bad for morale, especially at this dire juncture.

He leaned against the wall about a foot to the left of the door, waiting. When his quarry exited, he would not see the General there until it was too late.

The door slid open, and Captain Hirata Catigiri stepped out, wiping sweat from his brow. His eyes conveyed a sense of relief to be out of the room's sauna-like atmosphere. As he turned to the right, he froze when he felt static in the air and an ungloved finger pressed to his back. He knew better than to run; he would not get very far if he tried.

"For someone who never says anything, you've certainly been very chatty, haven't you, Captain?" Tsujimori said.

Hirata was too young to have seen active military duty during World War II, but he still knew a thing or two about basic strategy, which meant he knew when to fight and when to surrender. General Tsujimori was his superior not only in rank, but in ability. The man could literally slay monsters with his bare hands. Hirata stood no chance in a fight against him, especially not here, in the hallway of a ship lined with conductive metal.

Besides, he knew the full extent of his actions. The General, on the other hand, did not.

Hirata raised his hands slowly in surrender, then turned his head to look behind him at the General. He remained as silent as ever but motioned with his eyes back to the conference room.

Tsujimori had worked with Hirata long enough to know every nuance of the Captain's wordless forms of communication. Although rumors abounded as to why, ranging from a tragic accident to a religious vow of silence, the truth was that he was simply born mute. Few people had expected much from him because of this, but he had proven himself many times over throughout the years. His nonverbal ways of communicating did wonders for covert operations.

At the moment, it was clear he wanted to show the General something important in the private conference room, something which he seemed to think would explain everything.

Tsujimori nodded. "Very well," he said as he stepped aside, though he kept his ungloved hand raised and charged. "Show me what you've been doing, but remember that you're as powerless against me in there as you are out here."

Hirata nodded, for he knew it was true, and led the way.

Within the room, in addition to a video system, there was a series of keyboards set up for silent text communication between stations. Hirata sat at one of these and began typing.

<May I ask how you found out, Sir?> he typed.

The General read the words, still keeping his aim fixed on the traitor. "Good old fashioned detective work, as our American friends would say," he replied. "You almost never leave the ship, and you have clearance to use these spaces. Now, do you admit that you were telling Michael Sun about Richard Godfrey?"

<I confess,> the Captain typed, <but that does not mean I have betrayed you.>

"Oh?" Tsujimori scoffed. "You consider disobeying orders, acting in secret, and putting our entire operation at risk an act of loyalty, then?"

<With all due respect, Sir, isn't that what you've done in regards to bringing Godfrey-san aboard as well?>

Tsujimori had not expected that response, and even more unexpected was the fact that the young Captain made an excellent point. The plan on which Godfrey's involvement hinged reeked of treachery when viewed in a certain light. Past events in General Tsujimori's life put things in a slightly different perspective, however. Treason could be a virtuous act, but only if done for the right reasons. "Everything we have done is for the greater good," he said. "Just as it has always been."

<I know, Sir. You set an excellent example for all of us, and I follow it closer than you realize.>

Hirata reached for another keyboard slowly, so as not to invite an unwanted electric shock. He typed a sequence of numbers, and one of the video monitors flickered to life with a satellite image identified as a replay of events from three hours ago, indicated by the timestamp. The video showed a bus in a desert being attacked by Kaiju.

The General watched as the creatures tore the bus to shreds while letting the passengers flee, only to turn their attention to a small, familiar man who had exited last. Curiosity gave way to recognition as he saw the man was Michael Sun, then recognition turned to awe when Armadagger appeared and saved him from the attacking ceratopsians.

<Not only was I telling Michael-san about Godfrey-san, I was obscuring Armadagger's movements from the team so the event you see before you could happen,> Hirata typed.

Tsujimori was awestruck by the sight, but not so much that he did not ask the immediately obvious question. "How on Earth could you have known this would happen?"

Hirata hesitated, his eyes involuntarily darting back and forth as he tried to think of an answer. <That doesn't matter right now,> he typed. <What matters is the result. Michael-san is our public voice to the nations of the world. He needed to be on our side and understand everything. Now he does.>

The General eyed the Captain suspiciously. "You're sure of that?"

<I just spoke to him at Groom Lake. Trust me, Sir, he's a believer now. He supports the plan and everything we're trying to do.>

General Tsujimori nodded slowly as he scrutinized Hirata's face, which was reflected from every angle in the surrounding monitors. Just because the Captain was silent did not mean he was stoic. Any sign of dishonesty would have registered somehow, maybe as a bead of sweat or a twitch of the eye.

No such signs manifested.

Satisfied, Tsujimori put his glove back on. "Well, finally some *good* news from Groom Lake."

<Not entirely good, Sir. As always, some things remain beyond our control.>

"Such as?"

<The attacks are forcing the military's hand, Sir. Unless Michael-san can persuade them, they will be launching the machine the next time any of the Daikaiju appear.>

The General was out the door before Hirata even had time to turn around.

If there was one thing Michael Sun hated more than being at Groom Lake, it was being at Groom Lake with Sam Sigma, Head of Research and Development.

Every single aspect of Sam mixed perfectly into a cocktail of detestability. His slicked-back hair, his rat-like face, his pallid complexion, and the haughtiness that constantly radiated from his eyes like the ultraviolet rays of a dying star all congealed to make someone who Mike assumed could only have been loved by his own mother, and even she might have had a hard time of it. Worst of all was that Sigma knew how easy he was to despise, and he enjoyed it. He actually liked that everyone hated him, and why not? He held the most powerful position at the government's most clandestine top secret facility. What point did friends serve in such a life as his? It gave Sigma a weird satisfaction to know that no matter what everyone else thought of him, they still had to follow his orders, and they could not complain about it to anyone – not even their own families – since Groom Lake did not officially exist. To Sigma, friends were equals, and he had no room in his life for equals.

The only reason Mike was in the same room as Sigma now was because a decision had to be made about the machine. Since it was designed for use by the armed forces, this was a military decision, which meant the final choice went to Colonel George F. Stingray. Mike and Sigma had to help him make that decision, essentially playing the respective parts of the angel and devil that appear on the shoulders of a cartoon character. All three were gathered in Stingray's on-site office, with the Colonel seated behind a lovely antique mahogany desk. Framed photographs of him shaking hands with Truman, Kennedy, and Johnson hung on the wall behind him, although pictures of his family were strangely absent. Sigma was also seated comfortably in one of the two armchairs facing the desk. Mike was the only one who stood.

"Neither of you have even seen a living Kaiju up close, let alone gone through what I just did!" Mike said. His veins were still pumping with adrenaline from his encounter with Armadagger, which unfortunately made him come across as a bit frantic. He knew this was working against him, yet he could not calm himself down. How could he, after being in the presence of a Daikaiju?

Sigma, in contrast, was maintaining his composure in that arrogant way only he could accomplish. "You've said that several times by now, Mike," he said. "How is that nugget of so-called wisdom relevant to our discussion?"

Mike resisted the overwhelming urge to punch his opponent in his smug teeth. "You just think they're animals, Sam, mindless beasts ruled by instinct. Our boys in Operation Red Dragon have always said otherwise, that the monsters are intelligent. I didn't believe them until today. I've finally come face-to-face with one, and let me tell you both, they were right! Those monsters can *think!*"

Sigma tapped his chin. "I know there's a psychological term for assigning human qualities to inhuman objects and creatures... Anthropomorphizing? Projection? I'm sure it's one of those two, or both."

"Oh, so that's your tactic? Make me look crazy?" As soon as Mike finished asking the question, he regretted it, as he had just given Sigma more ammunition to use against him.

"Well, given your current appearance and mannerisms," Sigma said, "you're clearly not thinking straight."

Mike slammed his fist hard on the Colonel's desk, imagining it was Sigma's head. "I've never thought more clearly in my whole life!" He turned to face the Colonel. "Stingray, you've seen the footage, read the reports, heard the testimonies! Kozerah, Andrea, Armadagger... They aren't our enemies!"

Stingray drummed his fingers on the desk in thought. "They've caused millions in property damage," he stated.

Mike was, perhaps, a bit too quick to counter the Colonel. "But they saved lives! Not just mine, but all of those people in Japan and Chile! Pair them with CIGOR, and that's four giant monsters we can count on to protect us!"

"Unreliable," Sigma interrupted, his voice bearing the same inflection it might have were he commenting on the weather. "Even if we assume that this delusion is correct, those monsters defend us at *their* discretion, not *ours*. We can't control them."

Mike turned sharply. "So?"

"So what's to stop them from turning on us?"

"Us being *better*, that's what!" Mike began pacing. "If we start behaving like we're *worth* protecting, they *won't* turn on us!"

Sam's eyes narrowed. "So, you're suggesting that mankind live in fear of vengeful gods who will turn on us if we don't do what they want?"

"Why not? Just two years ago, the world was on the brink of nuclear war! Bay of Pigs, remember? Cuban Missile Crisis? And for what? A different economic system? Maybe some humility before God is what mankind needs before we destroy ourselves!" He shot Sigma a dirty look, and his tone became more aggressive. "Lord knows there's no shortage of *trigger happy idiots* who would be more than willing to destroy the world so long as they got the privilege of pushing the button!"

Sigma finally stood and tried to meet Mike face-to-face, even though he was shorter than anyone else in the room. "Well, *I* say humanity has outgrown the need for gods, whether it's a man with a long white beard or an overgrown salamander! I also say the machine will prove that!" He turned to Stingray. "George, listen to me. You're a smart man, a cunning strategist, and most important of all, a protector of the people."

"Sycophant," Mike grumbled loud enough to be heard.

"So you know that your duty is to those people. We can't say the same for the monsters. They're *unreliable.* Mike himself all but said outright that they could destroy us just for stepping out of line."

Stingray chewed his pipe in thought. "And what about CIGOR? He's definitely agreed to defend us, has he not? No ambiguity about that. I was there when we made that alliance."

Mike was about to jump on this and use it to win Stingray over to his side, but Sigma beat him to the punch. "CIGOR still has a will of his own. He could turn on us without warning for any reason. The machine, on the other hand, would be *entirely under our control.*" Sigma leaned in close. "George, think of how much chaos there would be all over the world if the human race began to think it didn't have mastery over creation. Governments would collapse, anarchy would spread through the streets-"

"You don't know any of that!" Mike shouted.

"It's the same logic we apply to the UFO cover-up." Sigma straightened his posture again, his voice adopting the silky tones of a deceptive devil. "Of course, since President Johnson has given you full authority here, the choice is entirely yours, George. Far be it from me to dictate your actions."

The silence was deafening as Colonel George F. Stingray considered everything he had heard. "It *is* my choice," he finally said. "Currently, though, things are quiet, so it's not a choice I have to make immediately. I'll need some time to think, but I will take both of your concerns into equal consideration. By the time one of those things resurfaces, I'll have made up my mind about the machine."

He leaned back in his chair and glanced at the ceiling. "You know, I'm getting sick of calling it 'the machine' all the time, and I can't be the only one who is. Do we have a proper name for that bucket of bolts yet?"

Sigma nodded. "The original name Professor Toshiro used in his proposal has grown on me somewhat." He spread his arms as if envisioning the name plastered boldly on a theater marquis. "Panzer Indigo. It just has a nice ring to it, wouldn't you agree?"

"How close is it to being finished?"

"It is finished, actually. Finished, fueled, and fully armed to the teeth. It simply awaits your command."

"All right," Stingray replied. "Get Panzer Indigo fully prepped for launch." He glanced at Mike. "Just in case."

The Colonel left, and Sigma shot a triumphant smirk at Mike before following.

Mike remained where he stood, feeling utterly alone in his defeat.

Despite the Colonel's parting words, he could not shake the sinking feeling in his gut that the decision had already been made.

CHAPTER 15

Those who study mythology are liable to notice common threads running through the many legends of ancient cultures. Many folklorists and archaeologists have struggled to come up with rational explanations as to how these bygone civilizations, who were separated by thousands of miles and had no form of contact with each other, could have told such similar stories with so many of the same details generation after generation. One explanation – considered a fringe theory by most respectable men of science – is that these myths are not myths at all, but factual accounts of real history.

One of the more curious myths found all over the world is the one about reptilian entities living underground. According to these myths, the reptiles had made their home in vast subterranean caverns connected by a network of tunnels below the surface. Accounts of what this realm was like varied between cultures, running the full gamut from volcanic wastelands to buried tropical jungles. In some regions, it was not hordes of reptiles who dwelled beneath the surface, but hives of unnaturally large insects.

Dr. Daisuke Armitage knew that these accounts were not myths, but terrifying truths. The caverns were where the dinosaurs and bugs had fled eons ago to avoid extinction, and the tunnels were how they moved around the globe without being noticed by humans. He had been concerned about what dangers the tunnels might pose, and so he had imparted his knowledge about them to Operation Red Dragon when the organization was founded.

For a long time, it had been said by the Red Dragons' top scientists that, despite the plethora of dinosaurs who lived there, the island of Rabu Nii had no such tunnels beneath it.

Those top scientists had been very wrong.

Now that their master Allorex was awake and leaving Rabu Nii, dinosaurs from all over the planet were mobilizing, tunneling through the Earth's crust toward one particular location.

And they were not the only ones on the move.

In the South Pacific, roughly ten nautical miles east of the Ogasawara Island chain, the United States Navy had posted a small fleet comprised of one aircraft carrier, two battleships, and a destroyer. It was a temporary post, more of a place to wait until a more strategic location was decided upon, but the ships were ordered to remain on full alert at all times. One never knew when the Russians might try sneaking a ship of their own through these waters.

Admiral William Smith, the man in charge of the little fleet, was pacing the bridge of the carrier. It was past midnight, but he could not sleep, especially not with news of the recent catastrophes in Chile and Japan. Reports were only now just reaching them. Most of his men assumed the statements about monsters attacking cities were part of some elaborate prank, akin to Orson Welles' fake *War of the World* broadcast from the Thirties, but Smith was not so sure. He had sailed the sea for a very long time, even before he had joined the Navy, and he had seen many unexplainable things over the years. Ergo, he had always accepted the idea that sea monsters – and, by extension, possibly other monsters – existed, though it was not an opinion he expressed openly as a military man.

To suddenly hear that monsters were not only appearing around the world, but were now said to be attacking cities, was disturbing enough to keep him awake.

"We have a bogie on radar, Admiral!" shouted the radar operator, a young corporal everyone simply knew as Hicks. "Five miles west!"

Smith put his personal thoughts and concerns aside, like any good soldier would do. Now was the time for action. "Speed and direction?" he said.

"Thirty knots, Sir," Hicks replied. "Heading straight for us. Should be visible by now."

Smith glanced out the window and saw the unmistakable lights of another vessel fast approaching his fleet. He raised his binoculars to his eyes and focused on them.

It was a submarine, fully surfaced and speeding towards them across the surface at an alarming speed. From this angle, the just-barely visible symbol of the hammer and sickle painted on the tower confirmed that it was Russian. A crewman – Smith could not discern his rank from this distance – stood halfway out of the hatch, waving his arms like a lunatic and shouting something in the fleet's direction.

"Orders, Sir?" asked Hicks.

Smith said nothing as he continued to stare, trying to figure out what was going on.

The sub drew closer. The entire fleet would be able to see it clearly now, and indeed, their spotlights were focused on it. The approaching enemy vessel continued on its course.

"Sir? Your orders?"

The radio crackled to life with the voice of Captain Jameson aboard the destroyer. "Admiral Smith? Enemy vessel approaching. Do we open fire? Perhaps a warning shot? Over."

Smith lowered the binoculars slowly and said, "Something's not right."

The sub came to a sharp and sudden halt, as though it had struck an invisible wall.

The Russian crewman moved in a blind panic, leaping from the hatch and diving into the water. He was followed by another man scrambling out of the tower in a similarly frightened state, followed by another, and another. The sub's secondary hatch opened, and more men poured from it. Terrified, they swam toward the American fleet.

Smith grabbed the radio, his mind finally made up. "Attention, all vessels! Attention all vessels! Hold fire! Do not engage! Ready life preservers and rescue rafts! Those men are in danger! Repeat: Those men are..."

His voice trailed off as he watched the water boil behind the Russian sub.

An enormous, sleek, oddly humanoid figure rose up from the sea. It was covered in smooth silver scales that shimmered with hints of a rainbow in the glare of the spotlights. Its head reminded Smith of a barracuda, but the muscular arms at its side betrayed the piscine image. With its mighty webbed hands, it gripped the fleeing submarine by the tail, and with surprising strength, lifted it from the water and tossed it away like a frustrated child chucking a baseball bat after losing a game.

Admiral Smith had no way of knowing it, but his fleet had come face-to-face with one of the Daikaiju who wished ill on the human race. Had a member of Operation Red Dragon been present at the time, they would have identified this leviathan as Barracudasaurus.

"My God in Heaven..." Smith whispered as he beheld the beast.

"Sir!" Hicks shouted. "Multiple contacts inbo-"

The sea erupted with a horde of monsters. The few Russians who had leapt into the sea were lost instantly in the churning chaos.

Admiral Smith remained transfixed in silent terror as he beheld the nightmarish spectacle. Though he was a military man, he had never encountered anything such as this before, and when confronted with the prehistoric vision before him, all of his years of training fled his mind, leaving him dumbstruck.

Refusing to wait for his orders, the other ships opened fire.

This only served to make the attacking creatures angry.

Smith was snapped from his stupor when the carrier rocked violently. His gaze drifted down to the deck, where an impossibly large alligator covered in spines and fins was hauling itself out of the water, a creature the Red Dragons identified as Wanirah.

Admiral William Smith did not see the end of the attack. He did not see the battleships as they were ripped apart by the jaws of ancient predators. He did not see the destroyer as it was crushed in the coils of a massive sea snake. He did not see the men under his command as they were devoured by prehistoric abominations.

All he saw was the inside of Wanirah's horrible mouth as it snapped down with tremendous force on the bridge.

"You're sure of that?" General Tsujimori asked as he stood on the *Akira*'s bridge, receiving the latest report.

The officer nodded. "We checked it twice, General," he said. "The scans indicated two red signatures when the fleet went down. Satellite images confirmed their identities."

X marched onto the bridge, Chakra trailing behind him, looking so incredibly happy that she practically floated to the radar station and settled in her chair like a feather. To the untrained observer, X would have still looked as stoic as ever, but those who knew him well would have noticed a subtle look of contentment in his eyes as well.

This expression vanished when he sensed the grave atmosphere surrounding Tsujimori and the young officer at his elbow. He approached the pair. "What's happening?"

"You mean while you two were busy?" Tsujimori asked, a hint of annoyance in his voice. He resisted the urge to continue on that thread, given the urgency of the matter. "Quite a bit, actually, but the most recent development is extremely disturbing." He dismissed the officer with a wave of his hand and turned to face X directly. "Barracudasaurus and Wanirah sank an American fleet just off the Ogasawara Islands, as well as at least one Russian sub."

The officer returned. "CIGOR just docked and printed his report. The Kaiju on Rabu Nii have left, and apparently…" He paused, nerves almost stopping his voice. "Allorex is guiding them."

With clear urgency and purpose, X and the General approached a wall on which was displayed a large map of the world. "Chakra," X said, his flat tone of voice barely masking his dread. "Display all red signatures, last known whereabouts."

Chakra, also concerned with what she had heard, typed a command into her keyboard, and the Pacific portion of the map lit up with seven red lights representing the Daikaiju.

X squinted as he thought. "Run a simulation: predicted destinations of all Daikaiju along the Pacific Rim based on current trajectories."

As Chakra typed the command, General Tsujimori adjusted his collar in agitation. "Even after Fukuoka and Chile, I still didn't expect it to all happen so quickly," he said, nerves tinging his voice.

X nodded slightly, though his eyes remained affixed to the map. "The world's in for a rude awakening, all right."

"Got it!" Chakra piped up, a hint of nervousness in her voice as well.

Trails of orange trickled from each red dot on the map like lava from a volcano, trailing along until they finally converged on a single point.

Every projected path led to Tokyo, Japan.

Everyone aboard the bridge spared but a single moment to be chilled to the bone. All at once, the Daikaiju were going to fight for supremacy in one of the biggest cities on the planet.

Not a single mind present could fathom the destruction that would befall Tokyo.

"Helmsman," X said. "Set a course for Tokyo. Take us right into the city."

The helmsman hesitated, uncertain if he had heard the command correctly. "Did you say we're going *into* the city, Sir?"

"My words exactly. Make it happen."

Still, the helmsman hesitated in carrying out the command. "Sir, the *Akira* is under strict orders to never come within sight of-"

"We are facing an extinction-level event, soldier!" X roared. He turned sharply and marched to the helm, his tall frame looming over the poor helmsman. In that moment, X almost looked like a Kaiju himself. "I don't care who sees us! I don't care if live video of the ship is blasted all over the six o'clock news! I don't care if Walter Cronkite wants to personally interview each and every one of us when it's over! This ship needs to be where it can do the most good!" His voice became that of a lion. "Get us over Tokyo NOW!!!"

CHAPTER 16

As the capital of Japan, Tokyo was one of the most recognizable cities in the world. On the evening of April 29, it would be rendered unrecognizable by the horrors of a bygone age.

Kyouske Sagara was bringing his fishing boat to port. He and his crew had been out to sea when the Daikaiju started appearing, though they had heard the reports on the radio of what was now being called the Attack on Fukuoka. Most of the crew found the news about monsters hard to believe, figuring instead that it was more likely some sort of attack by all-too-human perpetrators. Sagara remained wary. Not only was he a self-professed superstitious old sea dog, but he had seen a lot of unexplainable things in his time. Even on this latest excursion, he had seen large serpentine things in the distance heading in the general direction of the Japanese mainland. His men collectively agreed that the creatures were little more than whales and sharks. He let them continue to think that so they could keep working efficiently, but he silently knew that whatever they had seen, they were not mere run-of-the-mill fish.

According to the radio, which was playing as the ship headed for the shore, Tokyo was in the process of being evacuated under supervision of some international agency no one had ever heard of before called Operation Red Dragon. As a result, all vessels that normally docked in Tokyo Bay were being rerouted to different ports. Sagara was at the helm making the course corrections, but he was close enough to land to see the city.

Even from a distance, it was clear that something was wrong. There were explosions illuminating the evening sky, and the buildings were trembling like gelatin molds.

There was something else he saw, this time above the city. It was a floating object, which must have been huge to be visible from this distance. The shape reminded Sagara of a battleship, like the kind he had served on in the War so many years ago, and seeing such a vessel flying through the air was confusing to say the least.

What this floating ship was, Sagara had no idea, nor did he have much time to wonder.

A sudden jolt slammed Sagara's chest hard against the ship's wheel, knocking the air from his lungs and bruising his ribcage. He was dazed for a moment, vaguely aware of his men shouting outside the cabin, and the odd swaying of the ship which felt nothing like it should have on the water.

Had they hit something? Sagara had navigated these waters nearly his whole life, and knew of nothing in this patch of ocean which the ship could have possibly been caught on.

When his senses returned, he looked out at Tokyo once more, and was confused at how it seemed to have shrunk. From his perspective, it looked as though the buildings had somehow receded into the ground.

No, that wasn't right.

The buildings had not sunk. The boat had risen.

Sagara was stunned to see four silvery pillars rise up and surround his humble ship, water cascading off them in wide streams. The pillars curled inward, crushing the hull, blocking his view of the world around him.

The next thing he knew, his ship was flying through the air towards the city, straight into the gaping jaws of a creature he had only ever seen illustrated in books. It looked like some sort of gigantic dinosaur, and it leaped up to catch the boat like a dog catching a tennis ball.

The beast bit down hard on the bow, splintering it like matchsticks, but the cabin detached from the ruined hull and continued flying over it.

The last thing Kyouske Sagara saw in this material world was the side of a skyscraper fast approaching.

According to Daisuke Armitage, the land upon which Tokyo had been built held a special significance to the Daikaiju. According to legend, Japan had always been Kozerah's territory, and no matter where else on Earth he may have gone, he always returned to the island nation to rest and rejuvenate. Tokyo in particular had been one of the places where Kozerah had slumbered before rising to prevent the Huns from crossing the Sea of Japan. Challenging him to a fight there was a personal move on the part of his enemies.

Furthermore, Tokyo was densely populated by humans, whom Kozerah had always protected. Their deaths were sure to provoke him.

By the time the *Akira* had arrived, it was too late to avert disaster. The streets were already crawling with Kaiju. Massive lizards scaled up buildings, breaking into windows to claw at the terrified residents. Dinosaurs scoured the streets, eating or crushing every human they saw. The skies swarmed with insects shooting lasers from antennae and stingers, and the bay churned with sea monsters thrashing at every boat which drew near.

Even worse, the Daikaiju were with them. Allorex, Barracudasaurus, Exoskel, and Wanirah were all present. They commanded the chaos, pushing over towers in their paths, each roar the maniacal laugh of a dastardly villain.

*****

General Tsujimori stood at the threshold of the open shuttle bay, looking down at the hellish chaos raging below him. He had seen many battlefields of a similar nature, filled with opponents both human and inhuman, but the scale here was far more intense than anything he had encountered before. The Kaiju were attacking with the fury of Berserkers, not to mention that all four of their masters were present. There was nothing the General, or any human being, could do about the Daikaiju.

As much as he hated to admit it, Tokyo was lost. There was no point in trying to save the city anymore. The only thing left to do was make sure Tokyo was the only city these Kaiju ever got their claws on...assuming they could even make a difference in the fight at all.

At the very least, the evacuation order had been sent in time to clear the affected coastal part of the city. That was small but welcome consolation.

He glanced behind him, and saw X and Chakra standing by the *Kuroga*, sharing a deep embrace. Chakra was wearing a flight suit, which could only mean that she was finally getting her wish and officially joining them in battle. Either she and X had finally reached an understanding, or the situation was really that dire. Whichever it was, he welcomed her assistance.

Tsujimori closed his eyes and thought of his dear Saeko, trying to remember what her embrace felt like. He sighed as her vision wafted through his memory.

When he opened his eyes again, X was standing beside him. The sound of engines revving up echoed off the walls as the pilots prepared to launch into the fray.

There was no reason for Tsujimori to say anything, but he just could not resist the urge to take a jab at X, if only to alleviate the pre-battle tension. "So, did you kiss her, or are still you too shy to do that in public?"

X scowled at him. "Tell me, Ishiro, is your daughter still having identity issues?"

Tsujimori's face turned bright red. X only brought up his estranged daughter's unusual behavior if their verbal jousting struck a nerve with him. "Fine," he said. "Forget I said anything."

"Thank you." The guns snapped from X's sleeves into his hands. "Need a lift?"

"The last thing I want from you is a piggyback ride."

"Your choice. Mind the gap."

X leapt into the air and took flight.

General Tsujimori simply stepped over the ledge, an act accompanied by a burst of lightning from his entire body. The bolts arced and crisscrossed as they reached out for the metal in the surrounding buildings. Suspended in a net of lightning, he once again descended like an avenging angel.

The *Kuroga* and five shuttles retrofitted for combat followed close behind him.

Sumiko Tagaki clutched her infant son to her chest as she ran. She had been running since the attack began, not thinking of anything but protecting her child. How she had managed to avoid getting killed, she had no idea; all she knew was that she had to keep running until she could not run anymore...and she was approaching that threshold quickly. The muscles in her legs burned, and the infant grew heavier and heavier with each step.

Ahead of her was a section of the city which the monsters had not reached yet. She did not know if it was truly safer than what lay behind her, but she had to make it there.

She had to get to safety.

She could not.

Sumiko's legs buckled, and she twisted about as she fell, landing on her back so as not to crush her child.

She could not move. She could hardly breathe. The infant, jarred by the fall, began to cry.

From the corner of her eye, Sumiko saw a monster charging down the street towards her. It was a rattlesnake, an enormous one, fangs dripping venom. It stopped a block away from her and coiled, ready to strike. The chattering of its rattle echoing off the buildings made her skin crawl.

Sumiko clutched her wailing child tightly, shielding his eyes, whispering that he would be all right, that everything would be over soon.

Another chattering filled the air.

No, not chattering. It sounded more like gunfire.

Bolts of molten lead from the sky drove into the rattlesnake's body as it lunged, each rapid blow causing it to jerk about in midair unnaturally.

When the barrage was done, the serpent's head landed short of mother and child, slamming into the ground and laying there, lifeless.

A large black object, like a moth made of metal, descended and hovered above the dead snake for a moment, then flew off into the city to where the other titans rampaged.

Sumiko was so shocked that she did not even realize that she was still alive at first, nor that her baby had stopped crying, equally stunned by what had happened. She lay on the street, still catching her breath, still unwilling to move lest the dead snake suddenly spring back to life.

Another black object fell from the sky, landing beside her dramatically, but this was neither a ship nor a monster. It was a man, an American, clad in old fashioned clothing, armed with a pair of large handguns.

The foreigner helped her to her feet, and though her legs still hurt, she was able to stand once more. His glowing eyes locked with hers. "Go," he said in Japanese. "No monster will step beyond this point. I promise you and your child will live."

Without taking his eyes off of her, the man in black aimed one of his guns over his shoulder and fired. The shot sunk deep into the head of a charging dinosaur, which fell instantly. Its momentum carried its limp body forward until it skidded to a halt mere feet behind Sumiko's mysterious savior.

Sumiko felt every hair on her being stand on end as electricity filled the air. Bluish-white light drew her eyes towards the heavens, where she saw another man dressed as a soldier descending towards the streets. He was surrounded by arcing bolts of lightning which reached out to the buildings. He redirected a few bolts to incinerate a small cluster of grasshoppers which had leapt towards him.

"Run," repeated the man in black, and run she did.

Richard stood on the observation deck and stared at the carnage below, the odd recording stick he had been given capturing everything. Most of the city had been evacuated, but not all of it, and even from this height, he could still see the monsters below attacking the few defenseless people who had fallen behind in the evacuation.

Defenseless. That word definitely applied here. Richard had briefly wondered why the military had not responded to the attack yet, only to remember that Japan no longer had a proper military to respond with. There was a self-defense force, but it had far too many restraints in place to keep them from responding in time, and Richard had the distinct feeling that any regular military would be easily overwhelmed by the Kaiju anyway.

In short, Operation Red Dragon was on its own. This fight would see a single flying battleship, six advanced-but-still-puny fighter jets, and a trio of government-brand superheroes holding their own against a quartet of demigods and their prehistoric legions of untold thousands.

And here he was in the middle of it all, a reporter who could do absolutely nothing but bear witness to this madness.

Richard watched as the tiny resistance launched dramatically from the *Akira*, charging into a fray they knew they were not likely to win. It all seemed so unreal, more like a movie than history playing out before his very eyes

"Best seat in the house, don't you think?"

Richard jumped in surprise at the voice. It was Nancy, who had just entered. Although her question sounded as casual as ever, her voice carried some concern in it. She was clutching the cross on her necklace tightly.

Richard was surprised at this sign of concern until he realized that this experience with the Daikaiju was new for her as well. Indeed, how brave could anyone be in the face of Armageddon?

As the moment of surprise passed, he nodded. "I guess." His tone was even less confident than hers. "Do you really think the other Daikaiju will show up? Kozerah and the others?"

"I have no doubt of it."

"What makes you so sure?"

"Faith."

Richard frowned. "Faith in monsters like that? I find that a bit hard to buy into."

"It's no different than faith in God, if you ask me. The Daikaiju are just as unknowable and unpredictable, but they come through when we need them."

Richard looked at Nancy with inquisitive, skeptical eyes. "You believe in God? Like, the traditional Holy Trinity God?"

She nodded. "Yeah, among other things. It's gotten me through some pretty rough patches in my life."

Richard's eyes darted from Nancy's face to the cross around her neck. He had been wondering why she wore that, and now he had an answer. Even so, he shook his head. "That's great for you, Nancy, but frankly, I'm having a hard time reconciling all of this insanity about dragons and mutants with the Bible."

"You just haven't read the books they left out like I have," Nancy said. "Vatican Secret Archives, Section Fifty-four. Besides, after everything you've seen so far, is the idea of God really that outlandish?"

"Everything I've seen so far already *is* outlandish!" Richard exclaimed, and in so doing, he saw exactly what she meant. "Okay, I guess I get what you're saying. Nonetheless, Kozerah, Andrea, and Armadagger still aren't here yet."

Nancy pointed out the window. "No they're not, but *he* is."

Richard followed Nancy's finger, expecting to see X flying by.

Instead, he saw something completely new to him.

Marching across the top of the *Akira* as X and the General had done before, Richard saw something that looked to be equal parts machine and creature. The upright torso was covered in pale blue armor separated into three pieces, each of which met at the top in a thick upturned spike. This same pale blue metal also formed the entirety of its four limbs. At the ends of each arm, enormous pairs of scissor blades jutted out in place of hands, and dull silver hooks took the place of feet. From its back rose a pair of forward-facing membranes that looked like sails, and nestled between them was a large rocket that almost looked like something out of a cartoon. Any exposed skin was leathery and colored a rich but flat yellow. Swaying behind it was a tail as long as its body, at the end of which spun a circular sawblade.

The head was the strangest part of all. There appeared to be the beginnings of a natural dark-brown beak, but it was broken off in odd places, and the rest of it had been replaced with the pale blue metal, sculpted to match the missing organic parts and serrated at the edges. Over the top of its cranium, something like a helmet was fused to the skin, from which rose spikes arranged like the points of a crown. Over where the eyes should have been was a visor that glowed with a singular blue light that somehow conveyed a great intelligence.

Richard realized that he had seen this glowing blue eye before. "Wait a minute..." He thought back to the corridor where he had first seen the light. "Is that what was behind those doors with, uh, the letters on them?" So much had happened that he had forgotten what the letters had spelled.

Nancy nodded. "Yup. That's our ace in the hole, the only Daikaiju on the government payroll. He was torn to shreds when we found him in the Arctic, so we patched him up, and now he protects us in return. Behold the Cybernetically-Integrated Giant Ornitho-Robot, better known as CIGOR."

With a piercing metallic screech like the sound of a thousand church organs, CIGOR took to the air as the rocket on his back ignited, and then he did the impossible.

He grew.

CHAPTER 17

CIGOR landed hard on the pavement, crushing several Kaiju under his clawed feet. Now at his true height, roughly two-hundred and sixty feet tall, he stood equal to Barracudasaurus, who was greatest among his foes.

CIGOR's ability to grow and shrink at will was a natural part of his physiology, a power that the humans who had revived him still did not understand, especially since it defied the known laws of physics on nearly every level. He not only increased in size, but mass, and even the inorganic portions which now comprised so much of his body had adopted this power once they were attached. It was as though the governing forces of nature meant nothing to CIGOR.

This power's implications toward man's understanding of the universe aside, it was undeniably useful in a fight.

A few Kaiju snapped at his metal legs, but he paid them no heed. The armor on his body may have been manmade, but the alloy's strength intensified with his height, so he could not even feel the biting and clawing of the lesser beasts. His tail swayed behind him in a fashion similar to an angered cat, the spinning blade on the end slicing through any creature in its path.

Soon enough, the humans he resided with distracted the Kaiju, drawing them away to another part of the city, and they left CIGOR's thoughts entirely. The Kaiju were not his concern. He was a Daikaiju, a living demigod, as were the four titans who stood before him. He was here for them.

CIGOR took a step towards his enemies and struck a fighting pose, screeching a challenge at his enemies.

Exoskel replied by spitting a fireball from his strange mouth.

Instantly, a beam of blue light shot from CIGOR's visor, and spread out in front of him to form a wavering force field. The fireball exploded harmlessly against the energized wall.

CIGOR took another step and lurched forward. As though it had been pushed, the projected force field shot ahead of him, slamming into his opponents with incredible power and knocking them into nearby buildings, which collapsed and covered them in debris. Now too distant to be maintained, the shield dissipated into the air.

CIGOR took stock of his work. Barracudasaurus, Exoskel, and Allorex were down, struggling to pull themselves from the rubble.

He realized too late that Wanirah had avoided the attack by falling flat on the ground.

With shocking speed, the crocodilian leviathan lunged at him. His jaws snapped shut just shy of CIGOR's beak, but the momentum still carried him forward into a successful tackle. CIGOR stumbled backwards and extended his arms out straight to either side. The blades dug deep into the buildings which flanked him, slowing his backward descent enough for him to regain his footing and stay partially upright.

Wanirah was too close to twist his head around and bite his biomechanical foe, so he flailed his stubby arms about, clawing at CIGOR's armored torso. Sparks flew at each strike.

For an instant, CIGOR's eye changed from blue to blinding white, and a searing laser bolt flared and struck Wanirah in the chin. It was not enough to pass through him, but it burned, scorching the soft skin of the gator's underside. Wanirah fell back, half pushing himself away, half repelled by the blast, and landed flat on his belly in a protective stance.

Now believing the advantage to be his, CIGOR pressed his attack, firing an unending volley of pulsing white laser bolts at his foe. Though Wanirah's armored back protected him from serious injury, he was nonetheless pinned.

CIGOR might have been able to wear the beast down if a fireball had not caught him in the shoulder. Unprepared for the blow, he fell into a building which collapsed its full weight onto his back.

He had been careless in losing track of the other three. While Wanirah had been on the offensive, they had recovered.

Allorex charged, mouth agape, intent on taking a bite out of CIGOR. His sights were set on the cyborg's tail, which was clear of debris and resting limply on the cracked street.

Reacting as quickly as possible, CIGOR lifted his tail into a defensive poise just in time for Allorex to clamp his jaws on the spinning sawblade. The massive dinosaur instantly reeled backward, sparks flying from his mouth as the metal scraped at his teeth. He shook his head as the vibrations rang through his mouth with disorienting fury, but wasted little time before striking again, to similar effect.

With Allorex occupied, CIGOR began pulling himself out from under the rubble.

Barracudasaurus and Exoskel circled around him, ready to strike while he was still vulnerable.

They never got the chance.

A prehistoric chorus sang out from the ocean, silencing every Kaiju and human in Tokyo.

*****

On the *Akira*'s observation deck, Richard felt chills run up his spine as the sounds echoed across the city. The windows around him shook so violently he was afraid they might shatter, destroying the only barrier between him and the chaos below.

Nancy, on the other hand, smiled at the sound. She looked almost overjoyed to hear it.

Apparently, her faith had been rewarded.

CHAPTER 18

Michael Sun burst into the control room overlooking the hangar where Panzer Indigo was housed. Colonel Stingray and Sam Sigma were already there, the latter looking rather like a very satisfied eel.

"What are you doing?!" Mike shouted, not because he had to be heard over the mechanical cacophony in the hangar, but because he was angry.

"We're preparing to launch Panzer Indigo," Stingray said as though the matter were settled.

Sigma walked towards Mike, getting uncomfortably close simply so he could rub his victory in. "In case you haven't heard," he said, "Tokyo has gone from the world's most crowded city to Sir Arthur Conan Doyle's worst nightmare, so we're responding, just like the rest of the world expects us to do. Somebody has to save mankind from these monsters, wouldn't you agree?"

Mike was having none of it. He pushed Sigma out of his way with more force than was needed, knocking him into a standing coat tree with a thud which would have been more satisfying if Mike was not in a rush to prevent a disaster.

He ran to Stingray's side. "Colonel, we've got people there who are already responding! Operation Red Dragon can handle it, and the Daikaiju-"

"The Daikaiju don't share our interests, Mr. Sun," Stingray interrupted. His sunglass-shaded gaze remained transfixed on the giant robot beyond the observation window. "As for your Red Dragons, they're a freak show full of loose cannons."

Mike massaged his temples in frustration. "That's Sigma talking, Stingray! They'll protect us! I told you what happened earlier when-"

"Oh yes, *earlier*," Sigma snarled as he reentered the conversation. He was rubbing a part of his arm which had been bruised by his fall. "Your little fairy tale where you *think* the giant echidna protected you from the dinosaurs. And I suppose Kozerah is a friend to all children, right?"

"Shut up!" Mike yelled, then turned back to Stingray. "I'm telling you, Colonel, sending Panzer Indigo to Tokyo will just make things worse! You have to trust me!"

Sigma let out a short, sharp laugh. "Hah! Yes, trust him! Trust that human ingenuity means nothing against a bunch of mindless lizards and bugs! Trust that a bunch of science projects know more about the cosmos than the scientists who made them! Trust the inconsistent man who, just the other day, voiced his full support for the very thing he's now trying to stop!"

"And what are *you* in support of?" Mike shot back. "You just want this to happen so you can have more power! That's all you've ever wanted! Even if this crazy scheme does work, it'll start a new arms race, and as head of America's top secret weapons development program, you'll get to be in charge of it!"

"In your opinion."

The intercom buzzed to life as an electronic female voice crackled through. "Panzer Indigo prepped and ready to go. Awaiting permission to launch."

Mike took a step that placed him right in front of Stingray, obscuring his view of Panzer Indigo. "George," he said, his voice softer and filled with pleading. "Don't do this. Please."

Deafening silence filled the observation room. Colonel Stingray's brow furrowed as he thought.

He inhaled slowly, then exhaled just as slowly.

"If mankind's survival is to have any meaning at all," he said, "then we need to win it for ourselves."

He pressed the intercom button. "Permission granted. Launch Panzer Indigo."

Everything in Mike's perception became fuzzy as he fell into a nearby chair, defeated. He was barely aware of the massive robot rising up behind him. He refused to acknowledge Sigma's haughty smile. He was only somewhat cognizant of when Sigma and Stingray left for the command center.

As his senses returned to him, he found himself full of energy once more.

He ran out of the control room, knowing what had to be done. There was a chance it would get him charged with treason, but for the greater good of the world, it needed to be done.

He had to contact the *Akira* immediately.

Barracudasaurus waded into the water of Tokyo Bay, swatting a fighter from the sky as one might swat a mosquito, knocking it hard into the water. He barked – at least, the noise sounded like barking – three times, and the hundreds of monsters that lived in the sea swarmed around him.

Ahead, Kozerah and Armadagger broke the surface of the water, their emergence sending tidal waves smashing into the shore. Andrea flew overhead, her flock trailing behind her in an ever-swirling thunderous cloud. She ignored Barracudasaurus, passing into the city where the half-metal cyclops had regained its footing to re-enter the fray.

As Kozerah and Armadagger drew closer, Barracudasaurus roared a command, and his legions of sea beasts charged forward. This was a sacrifice, he knew, and a part of him hated to do it. Few, if any, would survive this assault, but it was necessary for victory. Besides, the oceans of the world were teaming with millions more of his subjects.

The Kaiju hit their enemies with everything they had, digging teeth and claws into reptilian flesh.

Armadagger was barely affected. His armor did its job perfectly, injuring any creature that managed to avoid getting swatted aside.

Kozerah had no armor, but no wound inflicted on him was too severe. Surface scratches, nothing more, each one healing instantly. No Kaiju that managed to score a hit on him evaded his own lethal strikes.

The water of Tokyo Bay ran dark red within minutes.

Barracudasaurus gave his enemies no time to recover from the onslaught. He was upon them instantly, moving with a speed that belied his tremendous size. He rammed his shoulder into Kozerah's chest, knocking him back. Simultaneously, his tail swept toward Armadagger, the vertical fin at the end scooping up water that shot in sharp bolts towards the synapsid's eyes. The cold, salty, blood-soaked impact stung, causing Armadagger to instinctively rear back and raise his hands to shield his face, exposing his unprotected belly.

One extra kick ensured that Kozerah was down, at least for a moment, then Barracudasaurus struck at Armadagger, his needlelike claws tearing at the exposed soft flesh over and over.

A shift in the water told him that Kozerah was recovering. Swift as the breeze, Barracudasaurus delivered a series of rapid fire punches to Armadagger's wounded underside, stunning him, then spun and leapt, driving a nasty right hook into Kozerah's jaw.

The advantage belonged to him.

He would win. He was sure of it.

A flicker of light caught his eye.

Kozerah's horns glowed brighter and brighter, and a matching glow shone from inside his mouth.

Barracudasaurus wailed as purple fire seared his silvery scales.

Steel groaned and concrete buckled as Andrea landed atop a building which, prior to that, had been untouched by the battle. A jet of flame poured from her beak, sweeping across the streets below to ignite any opponent who was not smart enough to flee. Her children were swarming through the air in a twisting cloud, grappling with the flying insects the same way they had done on the other side of the ocean.

Two strange things caught Andrea's eyes as she took in the battlefield. The first was the oblong metallic log floating above the city. Thinking about it, she had seen this thing before, though only from a distance, and never with so many sparks flying from it. Yet at each spark, an enemy fell.

Next was the newcomer, a fellow titan that she had not been expecting. He seemed to be made, at least in part, of the same stuff as the floating object and the towers that covered the battlefield. What remained of his flesh had an air of familiarity to it, yet Andrea could not quite place where she had seen his kind before. It was a memory from ages ago, long before the human-creatures came into being.

Whatever they were was unimportant. They were fighting her enemies, and that made them allies.

Purple light flared behind her. Kozerah and Armadagger were still in the water, and the former was unleashing his own fiery breath on Barracudasaurus. The fish-lizard ducked under the water to escape the terrible heat, then reappeared at the shore, leaping out like the fish that shared his name.

It was not quite a retreat. Barracudasaurus had not given up. He was hoping he would be followed, and he would regain the advantage with the support of the others.

Andrea sensed commotion beneath her. There were Kaiju scaling her perch, hoping to catch her off guard.

She dug her talons into the tower's roof and spread her wings to their full span, easily large enough to blanket a football field. She raised them slowly, the tightening of her muscles visible beneath her leathery skin.

With a sudden burst of speed, her wings came down, slamming against the sides of the tower. Hurricane-force winds shot towards the street, knocking most of her enemies back to Earth. The few that held on followed their fallen comrades when she flapped her wings again.

Andrea noticed a nearby black thing that looked like an insect made of stone wobble and spin as it was caught in the current. Sparks flew from its wings, and a large housefly burst into slime.

Andrea decided that the black stone bug was no threat to her, so she left it alone.

On the *Akira*'s observation deck, Nancy slammed her fist against the wall as she silenced her portable communicator. She had just spoken to Michael Sun, who had called her directly from Groom Lake. He had told her about the launch of Panzer Indigo, and she knew what a horrible mistake that was. All that would accomplish was the undoing of everything Operation Red Dragon had worked to accomplish.

On the other hand, Richard, who had only heard parts of the conversation, was clueless. "Hold on," he said. "What's a Pansy Indian?"

"Panzer Indigo," Nancy corrected. "A machine commissioned by the boys at Gr-" She cleared her throat, catching herself before she gave away too much about America's biggest secret. "That is, the boys in the *military*," she continued. "It's a robot designed to kill Daikaiju."

"I thought that was impossible," Richard said. "All I've heard since Kozerah showed up was how godlike the Daikaiju are compared to humans. Doesn't that mean a robot made by humans would be completely ineffective?"

Nancy tuned her communicator to radio her superiors. "That's the prevailing theory, but humankind doesn't like being told it's not in control. Even worse is that Panzer Indigo is programmed to kill Daikaiju indiscriminately."

She brought the device to her lips. "X, General, you there?"

"We're a little busy!" X growled. His voice was followed by a rumbling through the device, which was timed perfectly with a bright explosion somewhere out in the city.

"Panzer Indigo is inbound."

There was a two second pause before X responded with an urgent sounding, "ETA?"

"Soon. *Very* soon."

On the streets, X immediately terminated communication with Nancy and blasted like a Fourth of July rocket into the sky, shooting and slicing any bug that got in his way.

"Hey!" shouted General Tsujimori as he watched X's departure. "Where do you think *you're* going?!?"

In an instant, he was surrounded by a horde of vicious-looking Spinosaurs and bus-sized iguanas, all looking for a shot at killing him.

Tsujimori adopted a strong fighting stance as his fists crackled with electricity.

His eyes narrowed defiantly as he stared down his reptilian adversaries.

"Bring it on."

"I still don't see what the problem is," Richard said. "If manmade weapons can't hurt the Daikaiju, why not just let them deal with this robot? They should have no problem destroying it, right?"

Given that this was a serious emergency, the last thing Nancy wanted to do was answer more of Richard's questions, but making sure he understood what was happening was just as important as saving the world. In fact, the two went hand in hand. Even so, she had places to be. What could she say that would get the point across quickly and clearly?

A perfect analogy formed in her mind.

"Look at it this way, Richard," she said. "Suppose there are a bunch of spiders living in your home. You don't mind them, since they eat other bugs, so you leave them alone. Then, one night, an especially large, especially toxic one bites you while you're making dinner. How would you respond to that?"

"Easy," Richard said. "I'd kill each and every one of those little pests." An instant later, he got it, signified by his utterance of, "Oh...crap."

Nancy nodded. "Oh crap is right. If Panzer Indigo attacks Kozerah, Andrea, and Armadagger, and they make the connection that humans built him, they'll enact some Old Testament wrath on us. Now, as much as I'd love to stay and chat some more, I've got to get to the bridge. You may as well stay here. It's as safe as anyplace else on the ship right now."

With that, she left as quickly as she could.

Richard turned back to the window, watching the battle as it raged outside.

Mankind now faced extinction on two fronts: one by nature's hand, another by his own.

From where he stood, he had no idea how this could possibly end well.

CHAPTER 19

Armadagger stomped into the heart of Tokyo, the street cracking at his every footfall. Despite the wounds inflicted by Barracudasaurus which still trickled blood, he was as determined as ever to win the fight.

He broke into a jog, then a run, and finally leapt into the air and curled into a ball. The different segments of carapace on his body locked together like puzzle pieces, and the beast was transformed into a massive spike-covered wrecking ball.

He fell back to Earth, and his momentum carried his rolling body down the street, crushing and impaling enemy Kaiju beneath him.

Andrea swooped in from behind, releasing a stream of fire that incinerated any survivors, then gave an extra flap of her wings to propel Armadagger with greater speed into Allorex's exposed side. The spikes dug in, and the pair continued forward for several city blocks, none of which were left unscathed by the time they came to a halt. Clouds of debris rose into the air, causing the Red Dragon shuttles to swerve in order to avoid disaster.

Armadagger uncurled and stood, a mistake he regretted immediately.

In the blink of an eye, Allorex sunk his teeth into the fleshy part of Armadagger's upper arm. He came from behind, a smart move that made retaliation nearly impossible. The spiky beast could not reach over his shell, and his tail was too short to deal any serious damage in defense.

With great effort, Allorex swung his body around in a spinning arc, then opened his mouth, releasing his foe.

Armadagger was lifted off the ground for an instant, then stumbled as he returned to Earth, plowing into buildings and collapsing onto his back. In similar fashion to a turtle, he was now stuck, and though this would not suffocate him, it did leave his more vulnerable parts completely exposed.

Allorex charged, teeth bared, and bit down hard.

X came to a stop beside the *Kuroga*, which was hovering close to CIGOR as his scissor hands snapped at Exoskel. Chakra was aiming the *Kuroga*'s guns at the divide between the giant insect's thorax and abdomen, which had been theorized to be a weak point.

X had no time to wait and see if it would work.

He fired a shot at Exoskel's right eye. It probably did not do any real harm; to the insect, it most likely felt no worse than dust that could be blinked away. However, since Exoskel had no eyelids and thus could not blink, the irritation stunned him long enough for CIGOR to knock him aside with a roundhouse kick to the cheek.

Before CIGOR and Chakra could press their attack, X swooped in front of them. "The bug can wait," he said. "Panzer Indigo is inbound."

"Oh shoot!" Chakra exclaimed. "Are we gonna fight it?"

"If either of us do that, Chakra, it's an act of treason against the United States, and that'll be harder to justify than giving a journalist a front row seat to this wrestling match."

"Yeah, but if he attacks the others, we're *all* dead."

X nodded, silently cursing himself for letting his monitoring of the robot's construction fall to the wayside. He maneuvered up to CIGOR's eye level. "CIGOR, we need you to handle this. You're not subject to the Law like we are."

CIGOR chirped with an audible hint of doubt.

"That oversized refrigerator is programmed to attack every Daikaiju here. If he attacks you first, that gives us the moral high ground, and you can fight back."

CIGOR growled indignantly.

"This is all Sigma's doing, and you know it as well as we do," X said. "The whole of humanity shouldn't suffer for one man's misguided ambition."

Off in the distance behind the half-mechanical cyclops, X could see a faint glint of light against the black of the night sky, signaling the approach of the robot.

CIGOR slowly cocked his head to the side, thinking.

Both X and Chakra held their breath as they waited for an answer.

Without another word, he turned and launched into the sky, aimed right at Panzer Indigo.

"So," Chakra said over the com. "Wanna help me kill some bugs, honey?"

X grinned. "Thought you'd never ask."

It is a scientific fact that the muscles which open an alligator's jaws are far weaker than the muscles which close them. They are so weak, in fact, that an average human could hold a gator's mouth shut with his bare hands, if he were brave enough to get that close.

A similar principle applied even when the alligator in question was scaled up by several hundred feet.

Kozerah and Andrea had thrown themselves full into battle, and while the latter was engaged in fisticuffs with Barracudasaurus, the former was engaging Wanirah by keeping his enormous jaws sealed tight with his hands. The gator thrashed violently, his claws raking impotently against Kozerah's armored torso while his tail slammed into buildings. The sight was very nearly comical.

A fireball burst close to Kozerah's eye, making him flinch, though he did not release Wanirah. It kept him distracted long enough for Exoskel, who had recovered from CIGOR's kick, to charge, the tines of his spork-like hands jabbing at the red giant's side, which was not as well protected as his back and front.

Kozerah tried to turn, but Wanirah's thrashing was working against him, and the gator knew it. He struggled against his captor more fiercely than before, fighting his every attempt to turn his armored back toward Exoskel's onslaught.

Exoskel grew more fervent with each strike. It was working. He was drawing blood from the strongest of his foes. If Kozerah fell, the battle was all but-

The sudden sensation of talons digging into his shoulders interrupted Exoskel's thoughts, and before he knew it, he was in the air, being carried away and tossed by Andrea.

Determined not to be beaten so easily, Exoskel spat a fireball that clipped the Pterosaur's wing, sending her into a plummeting tailspin as she dropped him.

Meanwhile, Kozerah released Wanirah from his grasp with a judo flip. The crimson titan paused, taking heavy breaths as he prepared to fire his heat ray at his opponent's soft, pale underbelly.

Barracudasaurus was not about to give him that chance. The fish-lizard appeared from nowhere, slapping his fin-tipped tail against Kozerah's fresh wounds, then tackled him into a nearby skyscraper.

By this point, there were very few Kaiju left in Tokyo, but the Red Dragons were also dwindling in number. Since the masters had begun their struggle, things had only gotten worse, as not even the protectors of mankind were taking any special care to avoid friendly fire.

Panzer Indigo's arrival would not improve that.

As lightning flew from his fingers to scorch his prehistoric opponents, General Tsujimori shouted into his communicator. "All shuttlecraft withdraw to the *Akira* at once! There's nothing left for us to do now. Repeat, return to the *Akira* immediately!"

He stayed behind, eyes scanning the sky which now glowed red and orange from both the spreading fires and the rising sun.

The glint of metal above him signaled the location of the approaching machine.

It was already here.

To CIGOR's eye, Panzer Indigo was a ridiculous thing to behold, even compared to himself and Exoskel. It might have been his own bias, though; perhaps it looked perfectly fine to its makers.

The war machine looked exactly like a human made of metal. Its sleek body was a shiny, almost mirror-quality silver, broken up by thick lightning-shaped streaks of glossy indigo which created the illusion of a superhero costume. All it needed was a cape and the image would have been complete. The face was a set mask, sculpted with almost the same level of detail as a Bunraku puppet, only with a large shark-like fin in place of hair. The mouth – which seemed like a useless addition to CIGOR – was permanently twisted into a sadistic grin, and the deep-set, featureless, glowing white eyes bulged out slightly. CIGOR noticed that the eyes were distinctly almond-shaped, the corners set at opposing forty-five-degree angles. They reminded him of the Japanese humans' eyes. It was an oddly specific design feature, one he could not fathom the purpose of.

CIGOR knew that some humans regarded his kind as gods, and this machine had been built to kill them.

Man creating a god in his own image for the sole purpose of slaying gods.

It was a strange inversion that made CIGOR sick.

This false idol had to be destroyed.

Panzer Indigo paused in front of CIGOR, his frozen face making it impossible to read his intent. CIGOR did nothing as he hovered, waiting for the machine to make the first move.

Panzer Indigo raised his hands, extending his thumbs and index fingers the way humans did to simulate guns, and pointed them at CIGOR. Holes opened in his fingertips, and a burst of smoke from each hand was instantly followed by dull pain in CIGOR's body as the missiles fired by the robot impacted on his exposed skin

A second burst of smoke signaled another volley of missiles, but this time CIGOR put up his defensive shield. He flew forward, slamming his shield into Panzer Indigo's upright frame. The robot tumbled backward, regained control after three flips, and executed a diving kick to CIGOR's face.

CIGOR spun on impact, bringing his tail around to slice at the offending appendage with its sawblade.

Sparks flew, and the metal was scarred deeply.

Panzer Indigo had no reaction, for it could not feel pain.

It continued pushing the cyborg back down to Earth, not even noticing that a tiny ship and even tinier man had begun flitting around it.

CHAPTER 20

Armadagger was injured.

Badly.

He had been unable to prevent Allorex from sinking his teeth and claws into his unprotected abdomen. It was lucky that Exoskel had landed nearby, as the impact had distracted the massive dinosaur long enough for Armadagger to curl up and shift his center of gravity, allowing him to roll away and recover.

When he uncurled, he saw that things were looking dire. Andrea was down, the newcomer – CIGOR, if he had heard correctly – was fighting some strange metal thing in the sky, and most harrowing of all, Kozerah was bleeding.

This had to end soon.

He turned at Exoskel's chattering roar. The bug seemed to think that he had an easy target to kill, and given Armadagger's current state, he was probably right.

Armadagger had one shot at staying alive and turning the tide of battle. It was a long shot, not guaranteed to work, but he had to try it.

His only advantage was knowing that Exoskel always led his attacks by spitting a fireball to stun his opponents.

The bug did not disappoint.

Exoskel hocked his flaming phlegm and took a step to begin charging.

Just as the fireball was about to hit, Armadagger swung his fist in a backhanded strike, his built-in armored gauntlet connecting with the projectile and protecting him from harm.

Luck was with Armadagger in that moment.

The fireball flew back like a tennis ball, returning to Exoskel's mouth, where it lodged itself and burst.

The explosion engulfed the bug's head, and within seconds, his entire body was completely aflame. Exoskel panicked, flailing his limbs and slamming his body into buildings in the vain hope of smothering the fire.

Armadagger simply stood and watched as his opponent succumbed to the immolation.

Within a minute of the explosion, Exoskel slowed and finally collapsed, all the life having been burnt out of him.

At first, General Tsujimori was surprised when the swarm of giant orchid mantises which had surrounded him suddenly froze, screeched in abject terror, and fled with incredible speed. Indeed, every insect in Tokyo was fleeing in a panicked retreat. Even the flying bugs had pulled away from the murmuration of pterosaurs above him.

He heard Armadagger roar, and curiosity overwhelmed him. He had to see what had happened.

Arcs of lightning pulled him up the side of one of the few buildings which still stood. He settled on the rooftop and located the spiky synapsid.

Armadagger was standing over the burning corpse of Exoskel. He pushed over a hotel, and the debris smothered the flames.

Behind him, Andrea spread her wings and returned to the sky.

Victorious, almost psychotic laughter escaped General Tsujimori's lips as he drank in this glorious sight.

One down.

Despite a few close calls, CIGOR had managed to keep his battle with Panzer Indigo in the air, but he knew it could not last much longer. His rocket was starting to overheat, meaning he would have to land soon to prevent damaging it, but if he landed before the robot had been incapacitated, it was bound to attack the others.

An upward rush of air distracted him long enough for Panzer Indigo to land a solid uppercut to his chin, sending him spiraling once more.

Clearly, CIGOR had no choice. He had to land. He would simply have to engage Panzer Indigo on the ground.

Chakra pulled the *Kuroga* around in front of Panzer Indigo's head. The robot had no reaction, or if it did, she could not tell what it was.

After it had knocked CIGOR down, Chakra was seriously considering pumping bullets into the machine's eyes. They seemed about as fragile as any ordinary lightbulbs. If she could blind Panzer Indigo, it might retreat to Groom Lake. At the same time, she knew that directly attacking the robot herself could be considered an attack against the United States military, which could land her in serious trouble. Rumor had it the military had a formula on file which could permanently kill her, and if they did, treason was an excellent reason to test it.

Something behind Panzer Indigo's head caught her eye, and once she realized what was happening, it was already too late to avoid catastrophe.

Andrea swooped in behind the machine, her head lowered in similar fashion to a charging rhinoceros. She was diving fast. Very fast. So fast that Panzer Indigo had only just started to turn around when the gigantic blade atop the Pterosaur's beak pierced its shoulder and completely severed its left arm. Oil and grease poured from the robot's body like blood, spraying in an upward arc as Andrea slammed her wing like a fist at the machine, sending him careening away.

Chakra began to wonder why Andrea was attacking Panzer Indigo, whether she was protecting CIGOR or was just clearing the sky for her flock. She had no time to wonder for very long, though, since Panzer Indigo's foot kicked out as he fell, shearing off her ship's right wing. This would have been enough to send her into a tailspin, but Andrea's continued forward momentum brought a sudden rush of hurricane-force winds with it, sending the *Kuroga* tumbling out of control even faster.

Chakra felt her spine straining under the g-forces.

She blacked out.

Panzer Indigo fell like a blazing silver comet, knocking Barracudasaurus in the head before landing in an awkward sitting position atop a pile of rubble, his back leaning against an apartment complex.

He looked very much like a marionette whose strings had been cut seated upon a throne of crushed skyscrapers.

Kozerah approached the fallen machine, curiosity filling his mind.

This was something he had not expected. What was this thing, and where had it come from? It looked like a human, but was as large as him and made of the same stuff as the floating log that was raining fire on the enemy Kaiju.

It looked like it was trying to move, but its limbs sat at odd angles, broken and useless. Was this thing alive? Was it like CIGOR?

Barracudasaurus' warbling war cry drew him back to his original mission. The metal giant, whatever it was, did not require any more of his attention. Right now, there was a fight to win.

Kozerah turned sharply to face his foe.

By complete accident, his tail slammed into the metal giant's head, knocking it clean off its shoulders. The head landed with a loud thud on a street some fifteen blocks away. Without it, the body went limp as system after system shut down.

Panzer Indigo was no more.

In Groom Lake, Colonel Stingray glared at Sam Sigma, who was stunned by the defeat of the machine on which mankind's victory had depended.

"Care to explain to me how that happened, Sigma?" Stingray shouted, livid at the outcome.

Sigma cleared his throat before answering, just as baffled as everyone else. "I… Well, it was just a prototype."

Stingray jabbed his finger into Sigma's chest as he growled. "I'd strongly advise you to have a better explanation than that for the Press!"

A sadistic smile crossed Sigma's face. "I don't have to explain anything to the Press, George. I don't officially exist, nor does this entire facility. All anyone will know in the morning is that Panzer Indigo has US Military insignias on it, and that you signed off on its construction."

He gently pushed Stingray's accusatory finger aside. Between that and the Colonel's slack jaw, he knew he was in the clear.

His smile became even more insipid. "Good luck with that explanation, George. You'll need it."

He turned and left, seeing no reason to remain in the presence of a soon-to-be-disgraced colonel anymore.

Chakra blinked her eyes open, disoriented and uncertain about what had just happened. Had she died again? Her back did not ache the way it usually did whenever it was broken. She might have been lucky and skirted death this time, but she had no idea how. The last thing she recalled before blacking out was that the *Kuroga* was in a tailspin, and she was going to crash. What had happened?

As her senses returned to full functionality, she became aware of how cold it was, and that wind was whistling past her ears.

Then she realized that she was being carried.

She looked up, and there was X, trench coat billowing in the breeze, carrying her back to the *Akira*. Below, she saw the *Kuroga*, mostly intact save the missing wing, jutting out of a skyscraper like a discarded shuriken. The cockpit windshield had been shattered, and given where she was, she could guess what had happened while she was out.

Chakra melted at the thought as she snuggled up close to her husband.

One ship besides the *Kuroga* had stayed behind in spite of the retreat order, and it was piloted by Captain Hirata Catigiri.

Slowly, he lowered his shuttle close to the rooftop where General Tsujimori stood observing the progress of the battle.

The General pulled himself up onto the wing of the fighter and walked up to the cockpit, where he knelt down. With the last bit of energy he was willing to spare, he placed his bare hands against the fuselage and magnetized them.

"Back to the ship, Captain," he said through the com. "We've done all we can here."

The ship ascended.

General Tsujimori scanned the battlefield below. Yes, Exoskel was dead, and it looked like Panzer Indigo had been dealt with as well.

He was right. Mankind had done everything it could.

It was up to the Daikaiju now.

CHAPTER 21

"Should we pursue the bugs, Ma'am?"

Nancy weighed the helmsman's question in her mind. With Exoskel gone, the bugs had no one to coordinate their attack anymore. If left to their own devices, it was possible that a new master might rise from their ranks, and the problem would start all over again. That was just a theory, of course; no living human had ever witnessed the death of a Daikaiju before, so no one knew what happened in the absence of one. Destroying the bugs while they were weakened might be a wise move.

At the same time, though, the bugs were retreating. They could have stayed and continued attacking, maybe dispersed and rampaged elsewhere, but instead, they were fleeing as quickly as they could. That meant they were not a threat without Exoskel's guidance.

"Ma'am?" the helmsman asked again.

Nancy shook her head. "Keep firing at them until they're out of range, but don't go after them." She looked out the window at the city. "Once they're gone, keep blasting at the lizards, then follow the same policy once their masters are down."

Daisuke Armitage, who stood beside Nancy, gave her a bemused look. "You really have no doubt in your mind whatsoever that we'll be victorious, do you?"

She nodded. "None at all. We *will* win."

In spite of Nancy's confidence, victory did not exactly seem assured when one appraised the battlefield. Armadagger was wounded and had curled back up into an armored ball so he could heal, an act which effectively removed him from the fight. Worse than that, there were still three enemy Daikaiju in Tokyo, and at the moment, in spite of Exoskel's death, *they* were winning.

A well-placed tail swipe from Wanirah swept Kozerah's feet out from under him. Allorex darted in from behind, locking his teeth onto the red behemoth's neck. Kozerah thrashed as he was strangled, but the dinosaur did not release him. Meanwhile, Andrea and Barracudasaurus were at an impasse, each taking pot shots that kept missing their targets, neither one getting close enough to the other to do any real harm.

CIGOR, freshly recovered from his rough return to the ground, took all of this in, and determined where he could do the most good.

He leapt into the fray, his scissor-hands snapping wildly. The blades closed on Allorex's tail, cleanly slicing off the tip, which flew upward and impaled itself on a radio tower.

The dinosaur wailed in pain, releasing Kozerah from his chokehold.

Kozerah immediately punched his attacker in the snout. With Allorex dazed, he could catch his breath, or at least he could if Wanirah was not charging him, jaws agape.

CIGOR stepped in once more, catching the alligator by the throat in his blades. Wanirah's neck was too thick for even CIGOR's razor-sharp blades to slice all the way through, but he now had an idea of how to finish the gator off.

He craned his neck over to place his head inside Wanirah's gaping maw, then projected a force field down the gator's gullet.

Wanirah's body swelled like a balloon as the force field expanded.

Then he burst in similar fashion.

As bloody pieces of alligator rained on Tokyo, Kozerah rose and grunted at CIGOR in an expression of gratitude. At their feet, the remaining army of oversized lizards and snakes which had been the fallen Daikaiju's subjects fled into the water.

Two enemies down.

Now victory was within reach.

Allorex charged once more, leaping into the air from behind Kozerah, hoping to once again catch him off guard.

Without even turning to look first, Kozerah delivered a sharp backhanded blow to the dinosaur in midair, knocking him into a raging fire that scalded his scaly hide before he rolled out of it. Though he was still breathing, he would not be getting up any time soon.

Allorex was done. He just had to be finished off now. Kozerah and CIGOR approached to deliver their killing blows.

An anguished cry from Andrea, punctuated by the bursting of concrete and buckling of steel, caught their attention. The pterosaur had been caught by the leg, and Barracudasaurus was swinging her around like a child swinging a ragdoll, slamming her into the surrounding buildings.

Kozerah roared and charged to her aid.

CIGOR started to follow, but stopped when he noticed something from the corner of his eye, or rather a lack of something.

Where Allorex had fallen, there was now a gaping hole, into which his saurian subjects were pouring like water. The tremendous carnosaur was nowhere to be found.

For a moment, CIGOR hesitated to follow Kozerah and pondered his next move. Should he pursue the dinosaurs? Allorex was clearly not dead, meaning he could still pose a threat in the future when he inevitably recovered.

Then again, he and his forces were retreating. Their threat to the human race, at least for the moment, was neutralized.

CIGOR chose to let the coward run. The dinosaurs now knew what they were up against. It would be a long time before they tried to attack mankind again.

Kozerah drove his shoulder hard into Barracudasaurus' ribs, causing the fish-lizard to release his grip on Andrea, who went hurtling through the air for almost a mile before crashing hard on the pavement. With her out of the enemy's reach, Kozerah began his own attack.

He had not yet been allowed to really let loose on an opponent in this fight, as his foes had been tag-teaming him the whole time. They had been smart. He was the strongest Daikaiju on the battlefield, so his enemies' strategy had been to overwhelm him in an attempt to wear him down.

Now, though, Barracudasaurus was alone. His partners were either dead or fleeing, and his subjects were confined to the sea.

That meant Kozerah could finally unleash his full fury.

The titans sparred, throwing and blocking punches, kicks, head-butts, and tail swipes with reckless abandon. Despite their great size, the pair became a swirling blur of claws and teeth. Buildings burst around them. The ground heaved and buckled at every footfall. For a time, they seemed equally matched.

This illusion of equality did not last for very long.

Barracudasaurus threw his fist, only for Kozerah to catch it and flip him over his shoulder, slamming him against the ground. The red leviathan's horns glowed, and purple flame rained down from his mouth on the fish-lizard's prone form.

Barracudasaurus writhed as the heat blasted him. He flipped onto his stomach and tried to crawl away, only to find himself flying as Kozerah kicked him like a football. The next thing Barracudasaurus knew, he was upright once more, his arms caught between the blades of CIGOR's massive hands. The scissors cut in deep, slicing through skin and muscle to scrape against bone, and the points of the cyborg's armored torso dug into the fish-lizard's back.

Kozerah charged and spun, slamming the spiked club and the end of his tail against Barracudasaurus' kneecaps. He backed up, then charged again, lowering his head to drive his horns into his target's gut. They pierced deep beneath the ribcage.

CIGOR released his grip, and Kozerah took hold of his foe. With a burst of strength surging through his mighty muscles, he lifted Barracudasaurus above his head, and brought him down hard onto his extended knee, breaking the fish-lizard's spine with a sickeningly loud crack.

Barracudasaurus went limp.

Kozerah lifted him again, and threw him with all of his might back into Tokyo Bay, where he landed with such a tremendous splash that it flooded the streets with sea water.

Richard looked out at the bay.

Barracudasaurus was floating face down in the water, completely motionless. The gills on his neck, half-submerged in the water, were still moving, which meant he must still be alive, but the movement was slow and labored, as if every breath was a struggle.

The few sea monsters that had survived the arrival of Kozerah and Armadagger gathered around their fallen master, and in a manner shockingly reminiscent of pallbearers, they gently guided his body out to sea, leaving a swirling trail of blood behind them. Eventually, they vanished beneath the waves.

It was a solemn departure, and Richard was almost moved to tears by it. Though these creatures had wanted to destroy humanity, he now saw that they were, in a strange way, very similar to humans, at least in some regards.

His empathy for these would-be destroyers of his race was instantly forgotten as he saw Kozerah, Andrea, CIGOR, and Armadagger gather on the shore, also watching the procession.

Together, they roared triumphantly at the rising sun.

Their victory chorus shook the *Akira*, as well as every building in Tokyo which still stood.

Andrea was the first to depart, taking to the air with a single flap of her wings. She and her murmuration of Pterosaurs flew towards the sunrise, back to the tranquility of their nests in the mountains of South America.

Armadagger was the next to leave. He dug his claws into the ground and vanished deep into the Earth in a thick cloud of dust and rubble.

CIGOR flew back towards the *Akira*, shrinking as he did. To Richard, the combined effect of the cyborg's return with his size change made it seem like he had not shrunk at all. He disappeared from view beneath the observation deck.

Richard's eyes drifted back to Kozerah.

He was surprised to see the red leviathan was staring right back at him.

No, that was impossible. Kozerah could not possibly see him here on the observation deck. Perhaps he had simply watched CIGOR's departure. Maybe he was wondering if the *Akira* presented some sort of different threat to be neutralized before he left.

Yet, for all his rationalizing, Richard still felt like Kozerah was looking specifically at *him*. It made no sense, he would later admit, but very little about his life had made sense these past few days.

Whether Kozerah was looking at him or not, the behemoth eventually decided to leave. Without so much as a grunt, he waded into the water and eventually slipped beneath the surface without a ripple.

Elsewhere on the *Akira*, there was likely cheering and celebration at the victory, but on the observation deck, there was only Richard's sigh of relief.

He fell back against the wall and sank as the tension left his body, replaced with a sense of peace and calm.

At last, it was over.

CHAPTER 22

On the journey back to America, Richard kept his eye on the news by way of the *Akira*'s various media outlets. Every TV network, every radio station, every newspaper was abuzz with reports and speculation about the cataclysmic events that had rocked the Pacific Rim over the past few days, and a man named Colonel George F. Stingray was in nearly every report. Whenever Richard saw him on TV, sweat poured from the Colonel's body worse than Richard Nixon had during his debate with Kennedy as he was pelted with questions about the robot Panzer Indigo. In every appearance, he sounded as if he wanted to say something that would shift the public's focus elsewhere, but he was clearly bloodying his tongue. To Richard's trained reporter's eye, it seemed as though this Stingray was a scapegoat, someone upon which all of the blame for a public relations disaster was being heaped. No doubt there were other men out there who should have been sharing the scorn with him, but from the look of things, they were safely hidden away while this Colonel Stingray had been left bleeding in the water to attract the sharks.

Could this man and the secret he was keeping have any connection to that mysterious lake Nancy had accidentally mentioned that one time? Richard suspected as much, but he knew by now that he would have to wait for another day to find out for certain.

That aside, the Kaiju, Daikaiju, and Operation Red Dragon were now out in the open, their images now being seen in homes all over the world. Vietnam and the Cold War were no longer anyone's primary concerns. Just like that, mankind now knew that monsters were real, and they were far greater than anything previously imagined.

The whole time, Richard was keenly aware of the one theme uniting every report.

Fear.

The discovery of monsters, government conspiracies, or people with superhuman powers would have been enough to shock the world individually, but all three happening at once…Richard had to admit, it was terrifying to anyone on the outside of it.

If people knew what Richard knew about the Daikaiju and Operation Red Dragon, if he could explain it to them as someone for whom this was just as new and strange, but who had learned more by being in the thick of it, maybe they would not be afraid.

Well, perhaps they would be afraid no matter what, but they would also have a certain level of security knowing that not all of these strange new things were evil.

The shuttle in which he sat, similar to the one which had whisked him to the *Akira* in the first place, was flying high over the mountains that framed San Francisco Bay, not far from the Golden Gate Bridge. Although Nancy and Daisuke had accompanied him on the ride, they had been silent for most of the trip as they had listened to the news reports.

Now that they were over land, Nancy finally spoke to Richard. "Well, that's all for now," she said. "God knows it's not the end, but we should have a bit of a lull in kaiju activity for the time being. I don't suppose you have any other questions before we part ways, Richard?"

Richard started to shake his head in a negative answer, but then something struck him. It had been bothering him from the very beginning, from the moment he had found himself in the company of monsters and madmen, but up until this point, things had been too hectic and confusing for him to voice it. Now was his chance. "Actually, there is one last thing," he said, which was partly a lie; he still had many questions even now, but this was the only one that mattered at the moment. "Why me?"

"Pardon?"

Richard scratched his head as he articulated his question. "What am I doing here? Why show me all of this? You guys brought me into your crazy world of demigods and conspiracies, gave me all of this information about the monsters and the nature of the world, but now that it's over, what am I supposed to do? I mean, Operation Red Dragon is still officially classified, isn't it?"

A strange look glinted in Nancy's eyes. "Huh. You're right, we *are* still classified, and you're a civilian." She shook her head slowly. "Well dang," she said, her tone as flat as ever. "I guess that means I have to kill you."

Nancy reached into her jacket, and Richard panicked. "Wait a minute!" he shouted as he leapt from his chair to take shelter behind it. "What if I promise not to tell anyone? I know I'm a reporter, but I can be quiet! I swear!"

Nancy removed her hand from her jacket. Richard expected to see a gun.

Instead, Nancy held a pack of gum.

Richard remained motionless as he watched Nancy open the pack, pop a stick of gum into her mouth, and begin chewing. He blinked as his heart continued racing from the scare he had just been subjected to. "Wha-" he stammered. "What the- That wasn't funny!"

"Yes it was," Nancy said, a mischievous smile on her face. She extended the pack to Richard. "Want some? It's spearmint."

Richard simply stared at Nancy with an expression that silently conveyed his desire to call her a psychopath, along with several other incredibly rude and unflattering words.

"Anyway, that *is* a good question," Nancy said as she pocketed her gum. "You saw the news on the way here, of course. The world has been forever changed as of last night. Humanity now knows that gods walk the Earth, and let me tell you, Richard, they are terrified. They don't know what's going on. They don't know that some of the Daikaiju mean us no harm. They don't know about us and our role in things, and unfortunately, we can't say anything about it. Even though everyone knows about us now, we're still sworn to secrecy until the UN says otherwise." She shook her head. "God only knows how long it'll take the most stubborn bureaucrats in the whole world to make that call."

She raised her index finger and pointed at Richard. "You, however, aren't sworn to secrecy. We always knew something like this would happen one day, you understand. You can only keep hordes of giant city destroying monsters a secret for so long. It's kind of funny, really; at first, nearly all of us in Operation Red Dragon thought that all the monsters were a threat, too. Obviously, we changed our minds the longer we stayed the course, but that took years of research and patience. If the everyday people are scared and want something done about the Daikaiju, the governments of Earth will listen to them, not us."

She leaned back in her chair. "You're our new mouthpiece, Richard Godfrey. You know the truth, and you're a reporter, which means you're going to spread the good word for us. Sell it to the papers, go on TV, write a book...do whatever you think is the best way to disseminate the truth. You came highly recommended, after all." Nancy glanced ahead in the cabin to where Daisuke Armitage sat, writing his own notes on what had happened, before continuing. "Now that you've been in the belly of the beast, there's no one on the planet more qualified for the job."

All of this sunk in, and even though it made a kind of sense to Richard, a worrying thought struck him. "Won't that get me in trouble? Wouldn't every government in the world come gunning for me? I'm not a Red Dragon, sure, but if I'm spilling government secrets..."

"We've got your back," Nancy said, her words punctuated with a wave of her hand as if she were physically swatting the thought from Richard's mind like a fly buzzing around his head. "As you've seen, we're more than willing to toss the rulebook out the window when we deem it necessary, and we're in good with the most powerful creatures alive. Anyone who tries messing with you will regret it."

A gentle bump signaled that the shuttle had landed, and Nancy rose immediately to guide Richard to the door. "Besides," she continued, "it's not as though we're leaving you alone."

The hatch opened, and Richard was stunned to discover that the shuttle had landed in the very heart of San Francisco, on the helipad of a skyscraper which he could not immediately identify being atop it. There was a well-dressed man standing at the bottom of the ramp as though he were expecting the ship's arrival, which he no doubt was. He appeared to be Chinese, if Richard had to guess, and he wore a badge on his shirt which bore the emblem of Operation Red Dragon.

"Mr. Godfrey, I presume?" he said. "Michael Sun, Red Dragon liaison. I'll be keeping an eye on you from here on out."

As Richard nodded towards the newcomer, for he wasn't sure how else to acknowledge him, Nancy slapped him on the back and delivered her parting words. "That's your new assignment. Go forth and spread the new gospel, Richard Godfrey."

Once he had descended the ramp, the shuttle took off, leaving Richard and Michael Sun alone atop the building.

As Richard watched the shuttle depart, he considered the words Nancy had used to describe his task. Gods. New gospel. The good word. The whole thing sounded almost religious to him, and in a way, perhaps it was. Richard had, quite literally, been taken into the sky, shown wonders beyond his wildest imaginings, and had learned an awesome truth, which he was now going to impart to the people, almost like a…

Like a prophet.

The full importance of his task struck him, and the greatest clarity he had ever experienced filled his mind.

Yes, that was the best word to describe his new task. He was a prophet, one chosen to enlighten the masses. That was the real path he had begun so long ago when he first heard Daisuke Armitage's special lecture.

Richard Godfrey's spirit filled with purpose. Yes, he would report it. All of it. He knew in his heart that this was what he was born to do.

"I can only imagine how many UFO sightings they're causing right now," said Michael Sun as he watched the shuttle depart. "You still have the recording devices they gave you?"

Richard nodded, removing the odd recording stick from his pocket as he did.

"Good," Mike continued. "I've got the tech to adapt it for the rest of the world." He paused for a moment as he mulled something over in his mind, then he decided to voice his thoughts. "For the sake of full disclosure, Mr. Godfrey, I originally saw the act of bringing you aboard for this job as nothing short of treason, but over the past few days I've had my eyes opened. It's hard to get up close and personal with a Titan and not be changed."

That caught Richard's attention. "Were you in Tokyo?"

"Nevada," Mike replied. "I guess that's one of the many things we have to talk about."

EPILOGUE I

Nancy sat beside Daisuke Armitage, who stared out the window with that same stoic expression he always wore. They were both silent as the shuttle took off, and they were back over the open sea when Daisuke finally spoke.

"Since I wasn't present the whole time, I'm curious," he said. "Exactly how much does Richard Godfrey know about everything we're really doing?"

Nancy poured some tea into a cup and took a sip before answering. "He knows everything he needs to know in order to do his job. That's what matters."

"And when, if ever, will he learn the rest?"

Nancy shrugged. "Next time."

Neither of them knew that "next time" would come much sooner than either of them would have guessed.

EPILOGUE II

Somewhere in the deepest trenches of the Pacific Ocean, Barracudasaurus was alive, but he was healing far too slowly for his liking. He wanted to strike again. He wanted vengeance, and he wanted it now.

His subjects had brought him to a hidden place to heal. It was a building, similar to what the ancient humans might have built, except humans had not had a hand in making it. This structure was already old when the humans first walked the Earth. Also, it was ludicrously huge.

Only the beasts who roamed the seas knew this building existed, and they knew there was power there.

It was reasoned, then, that this power might help Barracudasaurus heal.

The mighty fish-lizard was carefully deposited at a gaping entryway that was large enough for him to fit through. His tail weakly swayed back and forth, which propelled him further inside.

Then he stopped suddenly.

A pair of massive eyes stared back at him from the darkness. They were glowing, and they glared at him maliciously.

Barracudasaurus tried to turn, a difficult task with two broken arms and a fractured spinal column.

Legions of tentacles lashed out from where the eyes watched, wrapped around Barracudasaurus' entire giant frame, and dragged him into the blackness.

Whatever dwelled in the structure was awake.

And it had plans of its own.

GLOSSARY

(The) *Akira*: A futuristic flying battleship designed in Japan and built in America. Serves as the mobile base for Operation Red Dragon.

Allorex: A dinosaur Daikaiju, overseer of the dinosaur Kaiju, and enemy of mankind. Identified by his nasal horn and appearance that resembles both an Allosaurus and Tyrannosaurus.

Andrea: The Daikaiju matron of pterodactyls and protector of mankind. Identified by a distinct horn on her beak.

Armadagger: An armadillo-like Daikaiju and protector of mankind. Identified by his spiky carapace.

Barracudasaurus: A reptilian-piscine hybrid Daikaiju, overseer of sea monsters, and enemy of mankind. Identified by his silver scales and pronounced underbite.

Captain Hirata Catigiri: A silent young soldier of Operation Red Dragon, often serving as General Tsujimori's right hand man.

Chakra: A young Japanese woman turned into a yokai by Unit 731 during World War II. Incapable of dying. Skilled pilot. Identified by her green hair and canine attributes (ears and tail).

CIGOR (Cybernetically Integrated Giant Ornitho Robot): Somewhat avian Daikaiju made into a cyborg. He is a protector of mankind. Identified by his mostly-mechanical body, including scissor hands and eye visor.

Colonel George F. Stingray: A military colonel stationed at Groom Lake to oversee the construction and launch of Panzer Indigo. Identified by his striking resemblance to Douglass MacArthur.

Daikaiju: Japanese for "giant strange beast". Refers to singular megafauna exceeding 100 ft. in height.

Doctor Daisuke Armitage: A stoic paranormal investigator of Japanese-American descent. Currently a consultant with Operation Red Dragon. Rumored to be immortal. Identified by his antiquarian attire.

Exoskel: An insectoid Daikaiju, overseer of insect Kaiju, and enemy of mankind. Identified by his spork-shaped forelimbs.

General Ishiro Tsujimori: A Japanese soldier experimented on by Unit 731 during World War II. Able to conduct and generate electricity. Currently a commander of Operation Red Dragon. Identified by his neatly-pressed uniform and purple gloves.

Groom Lake: A secret base where the United States government constructed Panzer Indigo, and possibly other things. Also called Area

51 or Dreamland. Not officially acknowledged by the government as of 1964.

Kaiju: Japanese for "strange beast". Refers to megafauna species under 100 ft. in height.

Kozerah: The most powerful Daikaiju on record and a protector of mankind. Identified by his red scales, razor horns above eyes, and spikes on his tail.

(The) *Kuroga***:** An experimental stealth fighter used by Operation Red Dragon. Name is Japanese for "black moth".

Michael Sun: The official liaison between Operation Red Dragon and all world governments and military units. Identified by his no-nonsense attitude.

Nancy Boardwalk: An American task marshal in Operation Red Dragon, mostly acts as X's right hand woman. Identified by her usually calm demeanor.

Operation Red Dragon: A covert task force put together by the United Nations to neutralize Kaiju attacks. Current members include General Ishiro Tsujimori, X, Nancy Boardwalk, Captain Hirata Catigiri, Chakra, Dr. Daisuke Armitage, and Michael Sun.

Panzer Indigo: A large humanoid robot made at Groom Lake. It was designed for the sole purpose of killing Daikaiju. Identified by a cheesy grin and purple highlights on its armor.

Rabu Nii: An island in the South Pacific where dinosaur Kaiju roam. Removed from all maps by Operation Red Dragon and declared a Q zone.

Richard Godfrey: A reporter specializing in accounts of the paranormal recruited by Operation Red Dragon to report the truth about the Daikaiju. Identified by his often bewildered state.

Sam Sigma: The head of Research and Development at Groom Lake. Identified by how utterly unlikable he is.

Tokyo: Capital city of Japan which served as a battlefield for the Daikaiju.

Wanirah: A crocodilian Daikaiju, overseer of reptilian Kaiju (not dinosaurs) and enemy of mankind. Identified by the strange horns and fins on his body.

X: An American cyborg soldier with enhanced healing engineered during World War II. Identified by his black trench coat and fedora. Currently a commander in Operation Red Dragon.

CHARACTER GALLERY

The following pages are drawings of the various Daikaiju and major human players of the story you have just read. This is about as close as I can get to visually realizing the images in my imagination. Yes, I am more of a cartoonist than an illustrator, but it is a style which I think fits the story perfectly. Who knows? This might make an excellent piece of animation one day…

(NOTE: The word "acerodactyl" on Andrea's page is a term I used to describe what kind of pterosaur she is. The name is derived from *aceros*, a genus of hornbill native to Southeast Asia, upon which her design is based.)

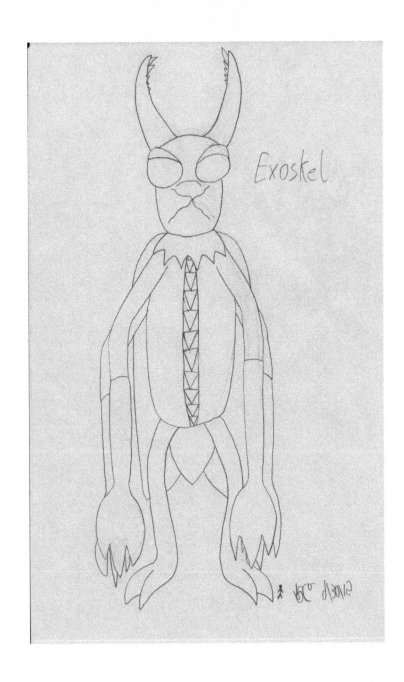

154

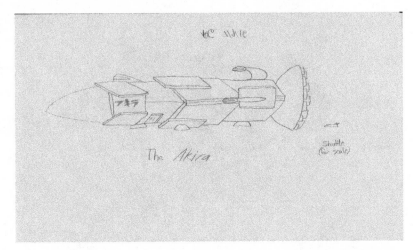

The *Akira*

Shuttle
(for scale)

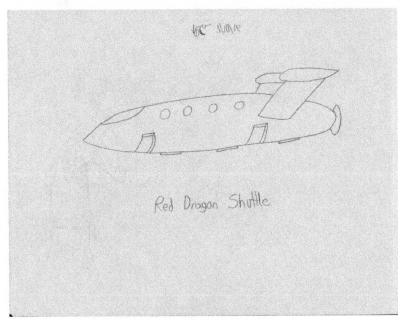

Red Dragon Shuttle

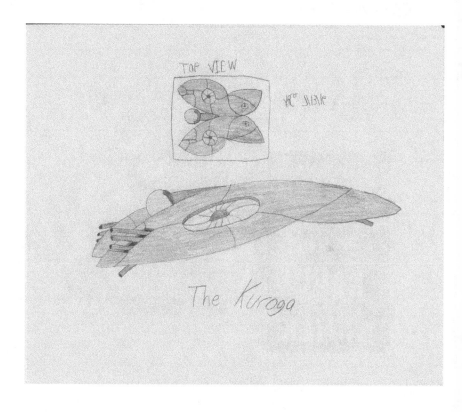

ABOUT THE AUTHOR

Although rarely photographed, eyewitnesses describe RYAN GEORGE COLLINS as a tall, hairy biped frequently seen wearing hats which went out of style when the Sixties began. A natural born entertainer and storyteller, he has devoted a large chunk of his life to theatrical performance, improvisational performance, puppeteering, and internet video production as the Omni Viewer. This book – inspired by his lifelong interest in *kaiju eiga*, paranormal investigation, and his Christian faith – is his first officially published work. He lives in Maine, literally minutes away from Master of Horror Stephen King, who has yet to return his calls.

CHECK OUT OTHER GREAT KAIJU NOVELS

KAIJU WINTER
by Jake Bible

The Yellowstone super volcano has begun to erupt, sending North America into chaos and the rest of the world into panic. People are dangerous and desperate to escape the oncoming mega-eruption, knowing it will plunge the continent, and the world, into a perpetual ashen winter. But no matter how ready humanity is, nothing can prepare them for what comes out of the ash: Kaiju!

RAIJU
by K.H. Koehler

His home destroyed by a rampaging kaiju, Kevin Takahashi and his father relocate to New York City where Kevin hopes the nightmare is over. Soon after his arrival in the Big Apple, a new kaiju emerges. Qilin is so powerful that even the U.S. Military may be unable to contain or destroy the monster. But Kevin is more than a ragged refugee from the now defunct city of San Francisco. He's also a Keeper who can summon ancient, demonic god-beasts to do battle for him, and his creature to call is Raiju, the oldest of the ancient Kami. Kevin has only a short time to save the city of New York. Because Raiju and Qilin are about to clash, and after the dust settles, there may be no home left for any of them!

CHECK OUT OTHER GREAT KAIJU NOVELS

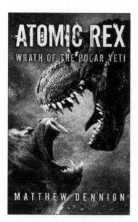

ATOMIC REX: WRATH OF THE POLAR YETI
by Matthew Dennion

It has been fifteen years since Captain Chris Myers used his giant mech to draw the kaiju of North America into each other's territory to have them destroy each other. Once all of the kaiju had battled to the death only Atomic Rex was left standing. In Antarctica, the kaiju known as Armorsaur has entered the frozen valley of the yetis and attacked them. Devouring all but one alpha male yeti who was exposed to the kaiju's blood and left dying in the snow. The yeti awoke to find himself transformed into a kaiju with an obsession to destroy Armorsaur. Chris and Kate are forced to protect the people of their settlement by drawing Atomic Rex into South America where he will battle the kaiju there to usurp their territory and claim their hunting grounds as his own. As Atomic Rex enters South America from the north the enraged Polar Yeti enters the continent from the south. The two most powerful kaiju in the world will battle their way through a multitude of giant monsters as they are set on a collision course with each other!

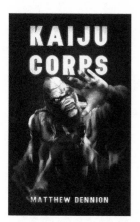

KAIJU CORPS
by Matthew Dennion

They are four soldiers who were genetically created to be mankind's last line of defense against potential world ending threats. They are soldiers who can transform themselves into gigantic monsters. They are the Kaiju Corps and they are facing a threat that is beyond the scope of even their fantastic abilities.

CHECK OUT OTHER GREAT KAIJU NOVELS

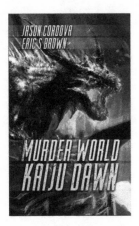

MURDER WORLD | KAIJU DAWN
by Jason Cordova
& Eric S Brown

Captain Vincente Huerta and the crew of the Fancy have been hired to retrieve a valuable item from a downed research vessel at the edge of the enemy's space.
It was going to be an easy payday.
But what Captain Huerta and the men, women and alien under his command didn't know was that they were being sent to the most dangerous planet in the galaxy.
Something large, ancient and most assuredly evil resides on the planet of Gorgon IV. Something so terrifying that man could barely fathom it with his puny mind. Captain Huerta must use every trick in the book, and possibly write an entirely new one, if he wants to escape Murder World.

KAIJU ARMAGEDDON
by Eric S. Brown

The attacks began without warning. Civilian and Military vessels alike simply vanished upon the waves. Crypto-zoologist Jerry Bryson found himself swept up into the chaos as the world discovered that the legendary beasts known as Kaiju are very real. Armies of the great beasts arose from the oceans and burrowed their way free of the Earth to declare war upon mankind. Now Dr. Bryson may be the human race's last hope in stopping the Kaiju from bringing civilization to its knees.
This is not some far distant future. This is not some alien world. This is the Earth, here and now, as we know it today, faced with the greatest threat its ever known. The Kaiju Armageddon has begun.

CPSIA information can be obtained
at www.ICGtesting.com
Printed in the USA
LVHW04s1451010518
575556LV00005B/963/P

9 781925 711790